THE BELGIAN TWINS by Lucy Fitch Perkins

Lucy Fitch Perkins was forty-eight when she was approached by a publisher friend who, impressed by her talents as both an illustrator and writer, which he knew through correspondence, urged her to write. He was so earnest that she thought of an idea for a children's book the next morning, and she immediately set to work making sketches and preparing the idea for presentation. The publisher came to dinner at their house the next evening and she showed him the idea. His response was immediate "go ahead and write it, and I want it". That book was The Dutch Twins, the first in what became a long running and wildly popular series. Here we publish another in the series 'The Belgian Twins'.

Index Of Contents

PREFACE

In this sad hour of the world's history, when so many homes have been broken up, and so many hearts burdened with heavy sorrows, it is comforting to think of the many heroic souls who, throughout the struggle, have gone about their daily tasks with unfailing courage and cheerfulness, and by so doing have helped to carry the burdens of the world, and to sustain other hearts as heavy as their own.

It is comforting, also, to know that there are many instances of happy reunions after long and unspeakable anxieties, adventures, and trials.

This story of two little Belgian refugees is based upon the actual experience of two Belgian children, and the incident of the locket is quite true.

The characters of the eel-woman and the mother of the Twins have also their living originals, from whose courage and devotion the author has received much inspiration.

CHAPTER I. THE HARVEST-FIELD

It was late in the afternoon of a long summer's day in Belgium. Father Van Hove was still at work in the harvest-field, though the sun hung so low in the west that his shadow, stretching far across the level, green plain, reached almost to the little red-roofed house on the edge of the village which was its home. Another shadow, not so long, and quite a little broader, stretched itself beside his, for Mother Van Hove was also in the field, helping her husband to load the golden sheaves upon an old blue farm-cart which stood near by.

Them were also two short, fat shadows which bobbed briskly about over the green meadow as their owners danced among the wheat-sheaves or carried handfuls of fresh grass to Pier, the patient white farm-horse, hitched to the cart. These gay shadows belonged to Jan and Marie, sometimes called by their parents Janke and Mie, for short. Jan and Marie were the twin son and daughter of Father and Mother Van Hove, and though they were but eight years old, they were already quite used to helping their father and mother with the work of their little farm.

They knew how to feed the chickens and hunt the eggs and lead Pier to water and pull weeds in the garden. In the spring they had even helped sow the wheat and barley, and now in the late summer they were helping to harvest the grain.

The children had been in the field since sunrise, but not all of the long bright day had been given to labor. Early in the morning their father's pitchfork had uncovered a nest of field mice, and the Twins had made another nest, as much like the first as possible, to put the homeless field babies in, hoping that their mother would find them again and resume her interrupted housekeeping.

Then they had played for a long time in the tiny canal which separated the wheat-field from the meadow, where Bel, their black and white cow, was pastured. There was also Fidel, the dog, their faithful companion and friend. The children had followed him on many an excursion among the willows along the river-bank, for Fidel might at any moment come upon the rabbit or water rat which he was always seeking, and what a pity it would be for Jan and Marie to miss a sight like that!

When the sun was high overhead, the whole family, and Fidel also, had rested under a tree by the little river, and Jan and Marie had shared with their father and mother the bread and cheese which had been brought from home for their noon meal. Then they had taken a nap in the shade, for it is a long day that begins and ends with the midsummer sun. The bees hummed so drowsily in the clover that Mother Van Hove also took forty winks, while Father Van Hove led Pier to the river for a drink; and tied him where he could enjoy the rich meadow grass for a while.

And now the long day was nearly over. The last level rays of the disappearing sun glistened on the red roofs of the village, and the windows of the little houses gave back an answering flash of light. On the steeple of the tiny church the gilded cross shone like fire against the gray of the eastern sky.

The village clock struck seven and was answered faintly by the sound of distant chimes from the Cathedral of Malines, miles away across the plain.

For some time Father Van Hove had been standing on top of the load, catching the sheaves which Mother Van Hove tossed up to him, and stowing them away in the farm-wagon, which was already heaped high with the golden grain. As the clock struck, he paused in his labor, took off his hat, and wiped his brow. He listened for a moment to the music of the bells, glanced at the western sky, already rosy with promise of the sunset, and at the weather-cock above the cross on the church-steeple.

Then he looked down at the sheaves of wheat, still standing like tiny tents across the field.

"It's no use, Mother," he said at last; "we cannot put it all in to-night, but the sky gives promise of a fair day to-morrow, and the weather-cock, also, points east. We can finish in one more load; let us go home now."

"The clock struck seven," cried Jan. "I counted the strokes."

"What a scholar is our Janke!" laughed his mother, as she lifted the last sheaf of wheat on her fork and tossed it at Father Van Hove's feet. "He can count seven when it is supper-time! As for me, I do not need a clock; I can tell the time of day by the ache in my bones; and, besides that, there is Bel at the pasture bars waiting to be milked and bellowing to call me."

"I don't need a clock either," chimed in Marie, patting her apron tenderly; "I can tell time by my stomach. It's a hundred years since we ate our lunch; I know it is."

"Come, then, my starvelings," said Mother Van Hove, pinching Marie's fat cheek, "and you shall save your strength by riding home on the load! Here, Ma mie, up you go!"

She swung Marie into the air as she spoke. Father Van Hove reached down from his perch on top of the load, caught her in his arms, and enthroned her upon the fragrant grain.

"And now it is your turn, my Janke!" cried Mother Van Hove, "and you shall ride on the back of old Pier like a soldier going to the wars!"

She lifted Jan to the horse's back, while Father Van Hove climbed down to earth once more and took up the reins.

Fidel came back dripping wet from the river, shook himself, and fell in behind the wagon. "U - U!" cried Father Van Hove to old Pier, and the little procession moved slowly up the cart-path toward the shining windows of their red-roofed house.

The home of the Van Hoves lay on the very outskirts of the little hamlet of Meer. Beside it ran a yellow ribbon of road which stretched across the green plain clear to the city of Malines. As they turned from the cart-path into the road, the old blue cart became part of a little profession of similar wagons, for the other men of Meer were also late in coming home to the village from their outlying farms.

"Good-evening, neighbor," cried Father Van Hove to Father Maes, whose home lay beyond his in the village. "How are your crops coming on?"

"Never better," answered Father Maes; "I have more wheat to the acre than ever before."

"So have I, thanks be to the good God;" answered Father Van Hove. "The winter will find our barns full this year."

"Yes," replied Father Maes a little sadly; "that is, if we have no bad luck, but Jules Verhulst was in the city yesterday and heard rumors of a German army on our borders. It is very likely only an idle tale to frighten the women and children, but Jules says there are men also who believe it."

"I shall believe nothing of the sort," said Father Van Hove stoutly. "Are we not safe under the protection of our treaty? No, no, neighbor, there's nothing to fear! Belgium is neutral ground."

"I hope you may be right," answered Father Maes, cracking his whip, and the cart moved on.

Mother Van Hove, meanwhile, had hastened ahead of the cart to stir up the kitchen fire and put the kettle on before the others should reach home, and when Father Van Hove at last drove into the farmyard, she was already on the way to the pasture bars with her milk-pail on her arm.

"Set the table for supper, ma Mie," she called back, "and do not let the pot boil over! Jan, you may shut up the fowls; they have already gone to roost."

"And what shall I do, Mother?" laughed Father Van Hove.

"You," she called back, "you may unharness Pier and turn him out in the pasture for the night! And I'll wager I shall be back with a full milk-pail before you've even so much as fed the pig, let alone the other chores, men are so slow!" She waved her hand gayly and disappeared behind the pasture bars, as she spoke.

"Hurry, now, my man," said Father Van Hove to Jan. "We must not let Mother beat us! We will let the cart stand right there near the barn, and to-morrow we can store the grain away to make room for a new load. I will let you lead Pier to the pasture, while I feed the pig myself; by her squeals she is hungry enough to eat you up in one mouthful."

CHAPTER II. THE RUMORS

When Mother Van Hove returned from the pasture, fifteen minutes later, her orders had all been carried out. Pier was in the pasture, the hens were shut up for the night, and the pig, which had been squealing with hunger, was row grunting with satisfaction over her evening meal; Fidel was gnawing a bone, and Father Van Hove was already washing his hands at the pump, beside the kitchen door.

"You are all good children," said the mother as she set down her brimming pail and took her turn at the wash-basin and the soap. "Jan and Marie, have you washed your hands?"

"I have," called Marie from the kitchen, "and supper is ready and the table set."

"I washed my hands in the canal this morning," pleaded Jan. "Won't that do?"

"You ate your lunch this noon, too," answered his mother promptly. "Won't that do? Why do you need to eat again when you have already eaten twice today?"

"Because I am hungry again," answered Jan.

"Well, you are also dirty again," said his mother, as she put the soap in his hands and wiped her own on the clean towel which Marie handed her from the door. She cleaned her wooden shoes on the bundle of straw which lay for the purpose beside the kitchen door; then she went inside and took her place opposite Father Van Hove at the little round oaken table by the window.

Marie was already in her chair, and in a moment Jan joined them with a beaming smile and a face which, though clean in the middle, showed a gray border from ear to ear.

"If you don't believe I'm clean, look at the towel!" he said, holding it up.

"Oh, my heart!" cried his mother, throwing up her hands. "I declare there's but one creature in all God's world that cares nothing for cleanliness! Even a pig has some manners if given half a chance, but boys!" She seized the grimy towel and held it up despairingly for Father Van Hove to see. "He's just wet his face and wiped all the dirt off on the towel. The Devil himself is not more afraid of holy water than Jan Van Hove is of water of any kind!" she cried.

"Go and wash yourself properly, Janke," said his father sternly, and Jan disappeared through the kitchen door. Sounds of vigorous pumping and splashing without were heard in the kitchen, and when Jan appeared once more, he was allowed to take his place at the supper-table with the family.

Father Van Hove bowed his head, and the Twins and their mother made the sign of the cross with him, as he began their grace before meat. "In the name of the Father and of the Son and of the Holy Ghost, Amen," prayed Father Van Hove. "Hail, Mary, full of Grace." Then, as the prayer continued, the mother and children with folded hands and bowed heads joined in the petition: "Holy Mary, Mother of God, pray for us sinners now and in the hour of our death, Amen." A clatter of spoons followed the grace, and Mother Van Hove's good buttermilk pap was not long in disappearing down their four hungry throats.

The long day in the open air had made the children so sleepy they could scarcely keep their eyes open through the meal. "Come, my children," said their mother briskly, as she rose from the table, "pop into bed, both of you, as fast as you can go. You are already half asleep! Father, you help them with their buttons, and hear them say their prayers, while I wash up these dishes and take care of the milk." She took a candle from the chimney-piece as she spoke, and started down cellar with the skimmer. When she came back into the kitchen once more, the children were safely tucked in bed, and her husband was seated by the kitchen door with his chair tipped back against the wall, smoking his evening pipe. Mother Van Hove cleared the table, washed the dishes, and brushed the crumbs from the tiled floor. Then she spread the white sand once more under the table and in a wide border around the edge of the room, and hung the brush outside the kitchen door.

Father Van Hove smoked in silence as she moved about the room. At last he said to her, "Leonie, did you hear what our neighbor Maes said to-night as we were talking in the road?"

"No," said his wife, "I was hurrying home to get supper."

"Maes said there are rumors of a German army on our frontier," said Father Van Hove.

His wife paused in front of him with her hands on her hips. "Who brought that story to town?" she demanded.

"Jules Verhulst," answered her husband.

"Jules Verhulst!" sniffed Mother Van Hove with disdain. "He knows more things that aren't so than any man in this village. I wouldn't believe anything on his say-so! Besides, the whole world knows that all the Powers have agreed that Belgium shall be neutral ground, and have bound themselves solemnly to protect that neutrality. I learned that in school, and so did you."

"Yes," sighed Father Van Hove. "I learned it too, and surely no nation can have anything against us! We have given no one cause for complaint that I know of."

"It's nonsense," said his wife with decision. "Belgium is safe enough so far as that goes, but one certainly has to work hard here just to make ends meet and get food for all the hungry mouths! They say it is different in America; there you work less and get more, and are farther away from meddlesome neighboring countries besides. I sometimes wish we had gone there with my sister. She and her husband started with no more than we have, and now they are rich, at least they were when I last heard from them; but that was a long time ago," she finished.

"Well," said Father Van Hove, as he stood up and knocked the ashes from his pipe, "it may be that they have more money and less work, but I've lived here in this spot ever since I was born, and my father before me. Somehow I feel I could never take root in any other soil. I'm content with things as they are."

"So am I, for the matter of that," said Mother Van Hove cheerfully, as she put Fidel outside and shut the door for the night. Then, taking the candle from the chimney-piece once more, she led the way to the inner room, where the twins were already soundly sleeping.

CHAPTER III. THE ALARM

For some time the little village of Meer slept quietly in the moonlight. There was not a sound to break the stillness, except once when Mother Van Hove's old rooster caught a glimpse of the waning moon through the window of the chicken-house, and crowed lustily, thinking it was the sun. The other roosters of the village, wiser than he, made no response to his call, and in a moment he, too, returned to his interrupted slumbers. But though there was as yet no sound to tell of their approach, the moon looked down upon three horsemen galloping over the yellow ribbon of road from Malines toward the little village. Soon the sound of the horses' hoofs beating upon the hardened earth throbbed through the village itself, and Fidel sat up on the kitchen doorstep, pricked up his ears, and listened. He heard the hoof-beats and awakened the echoes with a sharp bark.

Mother Van Hove sat up in bed and listened; another dog barked, and another, and now she, too, heard the hoof-beats. Nearer they came, and nearer, and now she could hear a voice shouting. She shook her husband. "Wake up!" she whispered in his ear, "something is wrong! Fidel barks, and I hear strange noises about. Wake up!"

"Fidel is crazy," said Father Van Hove sleepily. "He thinks some weasel is after the chickens very likely. Fidel will attend to it. Go to sleep."

He sank back again upon his pillows, but his wife seized his arm and pulled him up.

"Listen!" she said. "Oh, listen! Weasels do not ride on horseback! There are hoof-beats on the road!"

"Some neighbor returning late from Malines," said Father Van Hove, yawning. "It does not concern us."

But his wife was already out of bed, and at the window. The horsemen were now plainly visible, riding like the wind, and as they whirled by the houses their shout thrilled through the quiet streets of the village: "Burghers, awake! Awake! Awake!"

Wide awake at last, Father Van Hove sprang out of bed and hastily began putting down his clothes. His wife was already nearly dressed, and had lighted a candle. Other lights sparkled from the windows of other houses. Suddenly the bell in the church-steeple began to ring wildly, as though it, too, were shaken with a sudden terror. "It must be a fire," said Father Van Hove.

Still fastening her clothing, his wife ran out of the door and looked about in every direction. "I see no fire," she said, "but the village street is full of people running to the square! Hurry! Hurry! We must take the children with us; they must not be left here alone."

She ran to wake the children, as she spoke, and, helped by her trembling fingers, they, too, were soon dressed, and the four ran together up the road toward the village church. The bell still clanged madly from the steeple, and the vibrations seemed to shake the very flesh of the trembling children as they clung to their mother's hands and tried to keep up with their father's rapid strides.

They found all the village gathered in front of the little town-hall. On its steps stood the Burgomeister and the village priest, and near them, still sitting astride his foam-flecked steed, was one of the soldiers who had brought the alarm. His two companions were already far beyond Meer, flying over the road to arouse the villages which lay farther to the east. The church-bell suddenly ceased its metallic clatter, and while its deep tones still throbbed through the night air, the wondering and frightened people crowded about the steps in breathless suspense.

The Burgomeister raised his hand. Even in the moonlight it could be seen that he was pale. He spoke quickly. "Neighbors," he said, "there is bad news! the German army is on our borders! It is necessary for every man of military age and training to join the colors at once in case the army is needed for defense. There is not a moment to lose. This messenger is from headquarters. He will tell you what you are to do."

The soldier now spoke for the first time. "Men of Belgium," he cried, "your services are needed for your country and your King! The men of Meer are to report at once to the army headquarters at Malines. Do not stop even to change your clothing! We are not yet at war, and our good King Albert still hopes to avert it by an armed peace, but the neutrality of Belgium is at stake, and we must be ready to protect it at any cost, and at an instant's notice. Go at once to the Brussels gate of Malines. An officer will meet you there and tell you what to do. I must ride on to carry the alarm to Putte." He wheeled his horse as he spoke, and, turning in his saddle, lifted his sword and cried, "Vive le Roi!"

"Vive le Roi! Vive la Belgique!" came in an answering shout from the people of Meer, and he was gone.

There was a moment of stunned silence as he rode away; then a sound of women weeping. The Burgomeister came down from the steps of the town-hall, said farewell to his wife and children, and took his place at the head of the little group of men which was already beginning form in marching order. The priest moved about among his people with words of comfort.

Father Van Hove turned to his wife, and to Jan and Marie, who were clinging to her skirts. "It is only a bad dream, my little ones," he said, patting their heads tenderly; "we shall wake up some day. And you, my wife, do not despair! I shall soon return, no doubt! Our good King will yet save us from war. You must finish the harvest alone, but -" "Fall in!" cried the voice of the Burgomeister, and Father Van Hove kissed his wife and children and stepped forward.

Mother Van Hove bravely checked her rising sobs. "We shall go with you to Malines, at any rate," she said firmly. And as the little group of men started forward along the yellow road, she and many more women and children of the village marched, away with them in the gray twilight which precedes the coming of the dawn. The priest went with his people, praying for them as he walked, in a voice that shook with feeling.

The sky was red in the east and the larks were already singing over the quiet fields when the men of Meer, followed by their wives and children, presented themselves at the Brussels gate of the city.

CHAPTER IV. "FOR KING, FOR LAW AND LIBERTY"

At the gate they were met by an officer, who at once took command of the company. There was only a moment for hasty good-byes before the order to march was given, and the women and children watched the little column stride bravely away up the street toward the armory, where the uniforms and arms were kept. They followed at a little distance and took up their station across the street from the great doors through which the men had disappeared. There was little talking among them.

Only the voice of the priest could be heard now and then, as he said a few words to one and another of the waiting women. It was still so early in the morning that the streets of the city were not yet filled with people going to work. Only those, like themselves, concerned with the sad business of war were abroad.

To Jan and Marie the long wait seemed endless, but at last the doors of the armory sprang open; there was a burst of martial music, and a band playing the national hymn appeared. "For King, for law and liberty!" thrilled the bugles, and amidst the waving of flags, and the cheers of the people, who had now begun to fill the streets, a regiment of soldiers marched away toward the north. Jan and Marie stood with their mother on the edge of the sidewalk, eagerly scanning every face as the soldiers passed, and at last Jan shouted, "I see Father! I see Father!"

Mother Van Hove lifted her two children high in her arms for him to see, but Father Van Hove could only smile a brave good-bye as he marched swiftly past.

"No tears, my children!" cried the priest; "let them see no tears! Send them away with a smile!" And, standing on the edge of the sidewalk, he made the sign of the cross and raised his hand in blessing, as the troops went by.

For a time Mother Van Hove and the children ran along the sidewalk, trying to keep pace with the soldiers, but their quick strides were too much for the Twins, and it was not long before Marie said, breathlessly, "My legs are too short! I can't run so fast!"

"I can't too!" gasped Jan. Mother Van Hove stopped short at once, and the three stood still, hand in hand, and watched the soldiers until they turned a corner and disappeared from sight through the Antwerp gate of the city.

They were quite alone, for the other women and children had gone no farther than the armory, and were already on their homeward way to Meer. Now for the first time Mother Van Hove gave way to grief, and Jan and Marie wept with her; but it was only for a moment. Then she wiped her eyes, and the Twins' too, on her apron, and said firmly: "Come, my lambs! Tears will not bring him back! We must go home now as fast as we can. There is need there for all that we can do! You must be the man of the house now, my Janke, and help me take your father's place on the farm; and Marie must be our little house-mother. We must be as brave as soldiers, even though we cannot fight."

"I think I could be braver if I had some breakfast," sobbed Janke.

Mother Van Hove struck her hands together in dismay. "I never once thought of food!" she cried, "and I haven't a red cent with me! We cannot buy a breakfast! We must just go hungry until we get home! But soldiers must often go hungry, my little ones. We must be as brave as they. Come, now. I will be the captain! Forward march!"

Jan and Marie stiffened their little backs, as she gave the word of command, and, shoulder to shoulder, they marched down the street toward the city gate to the martial refrain, "Le Roi, la loi, la liberte," which Mother Van Hove hummed for them under her breath.

It was a long way back to the little farm-house, and when at last the three weary pilgrims reached it, they were met by an indignant chorus of protests from all the creatures which had been left behind. Bel was lowing at the pasture bars, the pig was squealing angrily in her pen, the rooster had crowed himself hoarse, and Fidel, patient Fidel, was sitting on guard at the back door.

Mother Van Hove flew into the kitchen the moment she reached the house, and in two minutes Jan and Marie were seated before a breakfast of bread and milk. Then she fed the pig, let out the hens, and gave Fidel a bone which she had saved for him from the soup. Last of all, she milked the cow, and when this was done, and she had had a cup of coffee herself, the clock in the steeple struck twelve.

Even Mother Van Hove's strength was not equal to work in the harvest-field that day, but she stowed the load of wheat which had been brought home the night before in the barn, and, after the chores were done at night, she and the Twins went straight to bed and slept as only the very weary can, until the sun streamed into their windows in the morning.

CHAPTER V. DOING A MAN'S WORK

When Jan and Marie awoke, their mother's bed was empty. "She's gone to milk the cow," cried Marie. "Come, Jan, we will surprise her! When she comes back from the pasture, we will have breakfast all ready."

"You can," said Jan, as he struggled into his clothes, and twisted himself nearly in two trying to do up the buttons in the back; "you can, but I must do a man's work! I will go out and feed the pig and catch old Pier and hitch him to the cart," he said importantly. "I must finish the wheat harvest to-day."

"Ho!" said Marie. "You will spill the pig-feed all over yourself! You are such a messy boy!"

"I guess I can do it just as well as you can make coffee," said Jan with spirit. "You've never made coffee in your life!"

"I've watched Mother do it lots of times," said Marie. "I'm sure I can do it just the same way."

"All right, let's see you do it, then," said Jan. And he strode out of the room with his hands in his pockets, taking as long steps as his short legs would permit.

When she was dressed and washed, Marie ran to the pump and filled the kettle. Then she stirred the embers of the fire in the kitchen and put on fresh coal. She set the kettle on to boil and only slopped a little water on her apron in doing so. Then she put the dishes on the table.

Meanwhile she heard no sound from Jan. She went to the kitchen door and looked out. Jan had already let out the fowls, and was just in the act of feeding the pig. He had climbed up on the fence around the pig-pen, and by dint of great effort had succeeded in lifting the heavy pail of feed to the top of it. He was now trying to let it down on the other side and pour the contents into the trough, but the pig was greedy, and the moment the pail came within reach, she stuck her nose and her fore feet into it. This added weight was too much for poor Jan; down went the pail with a crash into the trough, and Jan himself tumbled suddenly forward, his feet flew out behind, and he was left hanging head down, like a jack knife, over the fence!

It was just at this moment that Marie came to the door, and when she saw Jan balancing on the fence and kicking out wildly with his feet, she screamed with laughter.

Jan was screaming, too, but with pain and indignation. "Come here and pick me off this fence!" he roared. "It's cutting me in two! Oh, Mother! Mother!"

Marie ran to the pigpen as fast as, she could go. She snatched an old box by the stable as she ran, and, placing it against the fence, seized one of Jan's feet, which were still waving wildly in the air, and planted it firmly on the box.

"Oh! Oh!" laughed Marie, as Jan reached the ground once more. "If you could only have seen yourself, Jan! You would have laughed, too! Instead of pouring the pig-feed on to yourself, you poured yourself on to the pig-feed!"

"I don't see anything to laugh at," said Jan with dignity; "it might have happened to any man."

"Anyway, you'll have to get the pail again," said Marie, wiping her eyes. "That greedy pig will bang it all to pieces, if you leave it in the pen."

"I can't reach it," said Jan.

"Yes, you can," said Marie. "I'll hold your legs so you won't fall in, and you can fish for it with a stick." She ran for a stick to poke with, while Jan bravely mounted the box again, and, firmly anchored by Marie's grasp upon his legs, he soon succeeded in rescuing the pail.

"Anyway, I guess I've fed the pig just as well as you have made the coffee," he said, as he handed it over to Marie.

"Oh, my sakes!" cried Marie; "I forgot all about the coffee!" And she ran back to the kitchen, to find that the kettle had boiled over and put the fire out.

Jan stuck hid head in the door, just as she got the bellows to start the fire again. "What did I tell you!" he shouted, running out his tongue derisively.

"Scat!" said Marie, shaking the bellows at him, and Jan sauntered away toward the pasture with Pier's halter over his arm.

Pier had been eating grass for two nights and a day without doing any work, and it took Jan some time to catch him and put the halter over his head. When at last he returned from the pasture, red and tired, but triumphant, leading Pier, Marie and her mother had already finished their breakfast.

"Look what a man we have!" cried Mother Van Hove as Jan appeared. "He has caught Pier all by himself."

"He lifted me clear off my feet when I put his halter on," said Jan proudly, "but I hung on and he had to come!"

"Marie," cried her mother, "our Jan has earned a good breakfast! Cook an egg for him, while I hitch Pier to the cart. Then, while he and I work in the field, you can put the house in order. There is only one more load to bring in, and we can do that by ourselves."

By noon the last of the wheat had been garnered, and this time Jan drove Pier home, while his mother sat on the load. In the afternoon the three unloaded the wagon and stowed the grain away in the barn to be threshed; and when the long day's work was over, and they had eaten their simple supper of bread and milk, Mother Van Hove and the children went together down the village street to see their neighbors and hear the news, if there should be any.

There were no daily papers in Meer, and now there were no young men to go to the city and bring back the gossip of the day, as there had used to be. The women, with their babies on their arms, stood about in the street, talking quietly and sadly among themselves. On the doorsteps a few old men lingered together over their pipes. Already the bigger boys were playing soldier, with paper caps on their heads, and sticks for guns. The smaller children were shouting and chasing each other through the little street of the village. Jan and Marie joined in a game of blindman's buff, while Mother Van Hove stopped with the group of women.

"If we only knew what to expect!" sighed the Burgomeister's wife, as she shifted her baby from one arm to the other. "It seems as if we should know better what to do. In a day or two I shall send my big boy Leon to the city for a paper. It is hard to wait quietly and know nothing."

"Our good King and Queen doubtless know everything," said the wife of Boer Maes. "They will do better for us than we could do for ourselves, even if we knew all that they do."

"And there are our own brave men, besides," added Mother Van Hove. "We must not forget them! We are not yet at war. I pray God we may not be, and that we shall soon see them come marching home again to tell us that the trouble, whatever it is, is over, and that we may go on living in peace as we did before."

"It seems a year since yesterday," said the Burgomeister's wife.

"Work makes the time pass quickly," said Mother Van Hove cheerfully. "Jan and I got in the last of our wheat to-day. He helped me like a man."

"Who will thresh it for you?" asked the wife of Boer Maes.

"I will thresh it myself, if need be," said Mother Van Hove with spirit. "My good man shall not come home and find the farm-work behind if I can help it." And with these brave words she said good-night to the other women, called Jan and Marie, and turned once more down the street toward the little house on the edge of the village. Far across the peaceful twilight fields came the sound of distant bells. "Hark!" said Mother Van Hove to the Twins "the cathedral bells of Malines! And they are playing 'The Lion of Flanders!'"

The bells sang, and, standing upon the threshold of her little home, with head held proudly erect, Mother Van Hove lifted her voice and joined the words to the melody. "They will never conquer him, the old Lion of Flanders, so long as he has claws!" she sang, and the Twins, looking up into her brave and inspired face, sang too.

CHAPTER VI. AT THE CHURCH

Several days passed quietly by in the little village of Meer. The sun shone, and the wind blew, and the rains fell upon the peaceful fields, just as if nothing whatever had happened. Each day was filled to the brim with hard work. With the help of the Twins, Mother Van Hove kept the garden free of weeds and took care of the stock. She even threshed the wheat herself with her husband's flail, and stored the grain away in sacks ready for the mill. Each evening, when the work was done, the three went down the village street together. One evening, just at dusk, they found nearly the whole village gathered in front of the priest's house next to the church. Leon, the Burgomeister's oldest boy, had been to Malines that day and had brought back a paper.

The priest was reading from it to the anxious group gathered about him. "Oh, my children," he was saying, as Mother Van Hove and the Twins joined the group, "there is, no doubt, need for courage, but where is there a Belgian lacking in that? Even Julius Caesar, two thousand years ago, found that out! The bravest of all are the Belgians, he said then, and it is none the less true to-day! The Germans have crossed our eastern frontier. It is reported that they are already burning towns and killing the inhabitants if they resist. God knows what may be before us. Our good King Albert has asked Parliament to refuse the demands of the Germans. In spite of their solemn treaty with us, they demand that we permit them to cross Belgium to attack France. To this our brave King and Parliament will never consent; no true Belgian would wish them to. There is, then, this choice either to submit absolutely to the invasion of our country, or to defend it! The army is already in the field."

There was a moment of heavy silence as he finished speaking. Then the voice of the Burgomeister's wife was heard in the stillness. "Oh, Mynheer Pastoor," she said to the priest, "what shall we do? There is no place to go to we have no refuge!"

"God is our refuge and strength, my children," said the priest, lifting his eyes to heaven. "We have no other! You must stay here, and if the terrible Germans come, hide yourselves away as best you can, until they have passed by. Do not anger them by resisting. Bow your heads to the storm and have faith in God that it may soon pass over." He turned and led the way toward the little church as he spoke. "Come," he said, "let us pray before God's holy altar, and if the enemy comes, seek refuge in the church itself. Surely even the Germans will respect the sanctuary."

Solemnly the people filed into the little church, lighted only by the candles on the altar, and knelt upon the hard floor. The priest left them there, praying silently, while he went to put on the robes of his offices. Then once more he appeared before the altar, and led the kneeling congregation in the litany.

"From war and pestilence and sudden death, Good Lord, deliver us," he prayed at last, and all the people responded with a fervent "Amen."

That night, when she put her children to bed, Mother Van Hove fastened a chain with a locket upon it about Marie's neck. "Listen, ma Mie," she said, "and you, too, my little Jan. God only knows what may be before us. This locket contains my picture. You must wear it always about your neck, and remember that your mother's name is Leonie Van Hove, and your father's name is Georges Van Hove. If by any chance, which God forbid, we should become separated from one another, keep the locket on your neck, and our names in your memory until we meet again; for if such a thing should happen, do not doubt that I should find you, though I had to swim the sea to do it! For you, my Jan, I have no locket, but you are a man, a brave man, now! You must take care of yourself and your sister, too, if need should arise, and above all, remember this, only the brave are safe. Whatever happens, you must remember that you are Belgians, and be brave!"

The children clung to her, weeping, as she finished. "There, there," she said soothingly: "I had to tell you this so you would be ready to do your best and not despair, whatever might happen, but be sure, my lambs, nothing shall harm you if I can help it, and nothing shall separate us from one another if God so wills. Now, go to sleep!"

She kissed them tenderly, and, quite comforted, they nestled down in their beds and soon were asleep. She herself slept but little that night. Long after the children were quiet, she sat alone on the kitchen step in the darkness with Fidel by her side, and listened to the faint sounds of distant guns, and watched the red light in the sky, which told her of the burning of Louvain.

CHAPTER VII. THE TIDAL WAVE OF GERMANS

The next morning dawned bright and clear, and Mother Van Hove and the Twins went about their work as usual. The sunshine was so bright, and the whole countryside looked so peaceful and fair, it was impossible to believe that the terrors of the night could be true.

"To-day we must begin to gather the potatoes," said Mother Van Hove after breakfast. "Jan, you get the fork and hoe and put them in the wagon, while I milk the cow and Marie puts up some bread and cheese for us to take to the field." She started across the road to the pasture, with Fidel at her heels, as she spoke. In an instant she was back again, her eyes wide with horror. "Look! Look!" she cried.

The dazed children looked toward the east as she pointed. There in the distance, advancing like a great tidal wave, was a long gray line of soldiers on horseback. Already they could hear the sound of music and the throb of drums; already the sun glistened upon the shining helmets and the cruel points of bayonets. The host stretched away across the plain as far as the eye could reach, and behind them the sky was thick with the smoke of fires.

"The church! the church!" cried Mother Van Hove. "No, there is not time. Hide in here, my darlings. Quickly! Quickly!"

She tore open the door of the earth-covered vegetable cellar as she spoke, and thrust Jan and Marie inside. Fidel bolted in after them. "Do not move or make a sound until all is quiet again," she cried as she closed the door.

There was not room for her too, in the cellar, and if there had been, Mother Van Hove would not have taken it, for it was necessary to close the door from the outside. This she did, hastily, throwing some straw before it. Then she rushed into the house and, snatching up her shining milk-pans, flung them upon the straw, as if they were placed there to be sweetened by the sun. No one would think to look under a pile of pans for hidden Belgians, she felt sure.

Nearer and nearer came the hosts, and now she could hear the sound of singing as from ten thousand brazen throats, "Deutschland, Deutschland uber Alles," roared the mighty chorus, and in another moment the little village of Meer was submerged in the terrible gray flood.

At last, after what seemed to the imprisoned children like a year of darkness and dread, and of strange, terrifying noises of all kinds, the sound of horses' hoofs and marching feet died away in the distance, and Jan ventured to push open the door of the cavern a crack, just intending to peep out. Immediately there was a crash of falling tinware. Jan quickly drew back again into the safe darkness and waited.

As nothing further happened, he peeped out again. This time Fidel, springing forward, flung the doors wide open, and dashed out into the sunshine with a joyous bark.

In a moment more Jan and Marie also crawled out of their hiding-place after him. For an instant, as they came out into the daylight, it seemed to the children as if they had awakened from a dreadful dream. There stood the farmhouse just as before, with the kitchen door wide open and the sun streaming in upon the sanded floor. There were only the marks of many feet in the soft earth of the farmyard, an empty pigpen, and a few chicken feathers blowing about the hen house, to show where the invaders had been and what they had carried away with them.
Jan and Marie, followed by Fidel, ran through the house. From the front door, which opened on the road; they could see the long gray line sweeping across the fields toward Malines.

"The storm has passed," cried Marie, sobbing with grief, "just as Mynheer Pastoor said it would! Mother! Mother, where are you?" They ran from kitchen to bedroom and back again, their terror increasing at every step, as no voice answered their call. They searched the cellar and the loft; they looked in the stable and barn, and even in the dog-house. Their mother was nowhere to be found!

"I know where she must be," cried Jan, at last. "You know Mynheer Pastoor said, if anything happened, we should hide in the church." Led by this hope, the two children sped, hand in hand, toward the village. "Bel is gone!" gasped Jan, as they passed the pasture bars. "Pier, too," sobbed Marie. Down the whole length of the deserted village street they flew, with Fidel following close at their heels. When they came to the little church, they burst open the door and looked in. The cheerful sun streamed through the windows, falling in brilliant patches of light upon the floor, but the church was silent and empty. It was some time before they could realize that there was not a human being but themselves in the entire village; all the others had been driven away like sheep, before the invading army. When at last the terrible truth dawned upon them, the two frightened children sat down upon the church steps in the silence, and clung, weeping, to each other. Fidel whined and licked their hands, as though he, too, understood and felt their loneliness.

"What shall we do? What shall we do?" moaned Marie.

"There's nobody to tell us what to do," sobbed Jan. "We must just do the best we can by ourselves."

"We can't stay here alone!" said Marie.

"But where can we go?" cried Jan. "There's no place for us to go to!"

For a few minutes the two children wept their hearts out in utter despair, but hope always comes when it is most needed, and soon Marie raised her head and wiped her eyes.

"Don't you remember what Mother said when she put the locket on my neck, Jan?" she asked. "She said that she would find us, even if she had to swim the sea! She said no matter what happened we should never despair, and here we are despairing as hard as ever we can."

Jan threw up his chin, and straightened his back. "Yes," he said, swallowing his sobs, "and she said I was now a man and must take care of myself and you."

"What shall we do, then?" asked Marie.

Jan thought hard for a moment. Then he said: "Eat! It must be late, and we have not had a mouthful to-day."

Marie stood up. "Yes," said she; "we must eat. Let us go back home."

The clock in the steeple struck eleven as the two children ran once more through the deserted street and began a search for food in their empty house.

They found that the invaders had been as thorough within the house as without. Not only had they carried away the grain which their mother had worked so hard to thresh, but they had cleaned the cupboard as well. The hungry children found nothing but a few crusts of bread, a bit of cheese, and some milk in the cellar, but with these and two eggs, which Jan knew where to look for in the straw in the barn, they made an excellent breakfast. They gave Fidel the last of the milk, and then, much refreshed, made ready to start upon a strange and lonely journey the end of which they did not know. They tied their best clothes in a bundle, which Jan hung upon a stick over his shoulder, and were just about to leave the house, when Marie cried out, "Suppose Mother should come back and find us gone!"

"We must leave word where we have gone, so she will know where to look for us, of course," Jan answered capably.

"Yes, but how?" persisted Marie. "There's no one to leave word with!"

This was a hard puzzle, but Jan soon found a way out. "We must write a note and pin it up where she would be sure to find it," he said.

"The very thing," said Marie.

They found a bit of charcoal and a piece of wrapping-paper, and Jan was all ready to write when a new difficulty presented itself. "What shall I say?" he said to Marie. "We don't know where we are going!"

"We don't know the way to any place but Malines," said Marie; "so we'll have to go there, I suppose."

"How do you spell Malines?" asked Jan, charcoal in hand.

"Oh, you stupid boy!" cried Marie. "M-a-l-i-n-e-s, of course!"

Jan put the paper down on the kitchen floor and got down before it on his hands and knees. He had not yet learned to write, but he managed to print upon it in great staggering letters:-

"DEAR MOTHER

WE HAVE GONE TO MALINES TO FIND YOU.

JAN AND MARIE."

This note they pinned upon the inside of the kitchen door.

"Now we are ready to start," said Jan; and, calling Fidel, the two children set forth. They took a short cut from the house across the pasture to the potato-field. Here they dug a few potatoes, which they put in their bundle, and then, avoiding the road, slipped down to the river, and, following the stream, made their way toward Malines.

It was fortunate for them that, screened by the bushes and trees which fringed the bank of the river, they saw but little of the ruin and devastation left in the wake of the German hosts. There were farmers who had tried to defend their families and homes from the invaders. Burning houses and barns marked the places where they had lived and died. But the children, thinking only of their lost mother, and of keeping themselves as much out of sight as possible in their search for her, were spared most of these horrors. Their progress was slow, for the bundle was heavy, and the river path less direct than the road, and it was nightfall before the two little waifs, with Fidel at their heels, reached the well-remembered Brussels gate.

Their hearts almost stopped beating when they found it guarded by a German soldier. "Who goes there?" demanded the guard gruffly, as he caught sight of the little figures.

"If you please, sir, it's Jan and Marie," said Jan, shaking in his boots.

"And Fidel, too," said Marie.

The soldier bent down and looked closely at the two tear-stained little faces. It may be that some remembrance of other little faces stirred within him, for he only said stiffly, "Pass, Jan and Marie, and you, too, Fidel." And the two children and the dog hurried through the gate and up the first street they came to, their bundle bumping along behind them as they ran.

The city seemed strangely silent and deserted, except for the gray-clad soldiers, and armed guards blocked the way at intervals. Taught by fear, Jan and Marie soon learned to slip quietly along under cover of the gathering darkness, and to dodge into a doorway or round a corner, when they came too near one of the stiff, helmeted figures.

At last, after an hour of aimless wandering, they found themselves in a large, open square, looking up at the tall cathedral spires. A German soldier came suddenly out of the shadows, and the frightened children, scarcely knowing what they did, ran up the cathedral steps and flung themselves against the door. When the soldier had passed by, they reached cautiously up, and by dint of pulling with their united strength succeeded at last in getting the door open. They thrust their bundle inside, pushed Fidel in after it, and then slipped through themselves. The great door closed behind them on silent hinges and they were alone in the vast stillness of the cathedral. Timidly they crept toward the lights of the altar, and, utterly exhausted, slept that night on the floor near the statue of the Madonna, with their heads pillowed on Fidel's shaggy side.

CHAPTER VIII. GRANNY AND THE EELS

When the cathedral bells rang the next morning for early mass, the children were still sleeping the sleep of utter exhaustion. It was not until the bells had ceased to ring, and the door, opening from the sacristy near their resting place, creaked upon its hinges, that even Fidel was aroused. True to his watchdog instincts, he started to his feet with a low growl, letting the heads of Jan and Marie down upon the floor with a sudden bump. For an instant the awakened children could not remember where they were or what had happened to them. They sat up and rubbed their heads, but the habit of fear was already so strong upon them that they made no sound and instantly quieted Fidel. Again the door creaked, and through it there appeared a tall figure dressed in priestly robes. The children were so near that had they thrust their hands through the railing of the communion bank behind which they were concealed, they might have touched him as he passed before the altar of the Virgin and presented himself in front of the high altar to conduct the mass. His head, as he passed them, was bowed. His face was pale and thin, and marked with lines of deep sorrow.

"Oh," whispered Marie to Jan, "it must be the Cardinal himself. Mother told me about him."

The whisper made such a loud sound in the silence of the great cathedral aisles that Jan was afraid to reply. For answer he only laid his finger upon his lips and crept still farther back into the shadow. Fidel seemed to know that dogs were not allowed in church and that it was necessary for him to be quiet, too, for he crawled back with the children into the sheltering darkness.

There were only a few persons in the cathedral, and those few were near the door; so no one saw the children as they knelt with folded hands and bowed heads in their corner, reverently following the service as the Cardinal ate the sacred wafer and drank the communion wine before the altar. Later they were to know his face as the bravest and best beloved in all Belgium next to those of the King and Queen themselves.

When again he passed the kneeling little figures on his return to the sacristy, their lonely hearts so ached for care and protection, and his face looked so kind and pitiful, that they almost dared to make their presence known and to ask for the help they sorely needed. Marie, bolder than Jan, half rose as he passed, but Jan pulled her back, and in another instant the door had closed behind him and he was gone.

"Oh," sobbed Marie under her breath, "he looked so kind! He might have helped us. Why did you pull me back?"

"How could we let him see Fidel, and tell him that our dog had slept all night before the altar?" answered Jan. "I shouldn't dare! He is a great Prince of the Church!"

The sound of scraping chairs told them that the little congregation had risen from its knees and was passing out of the church. They waited until every one had disappeared through the great door, and then made a swift flight down the echoing aisle and out into the sunlight. For a moment they stood hand in hand upon the cathedral steps, clasping their bundle and waiting for the next turn of fortune's wheel.

The bright sunlight of the summer day, shining on the open square, almost blinded them, and what they saw in the square, when their eyes had become used to it, did not comfort them. Everywhere there were German soldiers with their terrible bayonets and pointed helmets and their terrible songs. Everywhere there were pale and desperate Belgians fleeing before the arrogant German invader.

"Oh, Jan," whispered Marie clinging to him, "there are so many people! How shall we ever find Mother? I didn't know there were so many people in the whole world."

"It isn't likely that we'll find her by just standing here, anyway," answered Jan. "We've got to keep going till we get somewhere."

He slung the bundle on his shoulder and whistled to Fidel, who had gone down the steps to bark at a homeless cat.

"Come along," he said to Marie. And once more the little pilgrims took up their journey. At the first corner they paused, not knowing whether to go to the right or to the left.

"Which way?" said Marie.

Jan stood still and looked first in one direction and then in the other.

"Here, gutter-snipes, what are you standing here for? Make way for your betters!" said a gruff voice behind them, and, turning, the children found themselves face to face with a German officer dressed in a resplendent uniform and accompanied by a group of swaggering young soldiers. Too frightened to move, the children only looked up at him and did not stir.

"Get out of the way, I tell you!" roared the officer, turning purple with rage; "Orderly!" One of the young men sprang forward. He seized Jan by the arm and deftly kicked him into the gutter. Another at the same moment laid his hands on Marie. But he reckoned without Fidel, faithful Fidel, who knew no difference between German and Belgian, but knew only that no cruel hand should touch his beloved Marie, while he was there to defend her. With a fierce growl he sprang at the young orderly and buried his teeth in his leg. Howling with pain, the orderly dropped Marie, while another soldier drew his sword with an oath and made a thrust at Fidel. Fortunately Fidel was too quick for him. He let go his hold upon the leg of the orderly, tearing a large hole in his uniform as he did so, and flung himself directly between the legs of the other soldier who was lunging at him with the sword. The next instant the surprised German found himself sprawling upon the sidewalk, and saw Fidel, who had escaped without a scratch, dashing wildly up the street after Jan and Marie. Beside himself with rage, the soldier drew a revolver and fired a shot, which barely missed Fidel, and buried itself in the doorstep of the house past which he was running.

If Jan and Marie had not turned a corner just at that moment, and if Fidel had not followed them, there is no telling what might have happened next, for the young soldier was very angry indeed. Perhaps he considered it beneath his dignity to run after them, and perhaps he saw that Jan and Marie could both run like the wind and he would not be likely to catch them if he did. At any rate, he did not follow. He picked himself up and dusted his clothes, using very bad language as he did so, and followed the officer and his companions up the street.

Meanwhile the tired children ran on and on, fear lending speed to their weary legs. Round behind the great cathedral they sped, hoping to find some way of escape from the terrors of the town, but their way was blocked by the smoking ruins of a section of the city which the Germans had burned in the night, and there was no way to get out in that direction. Terrified and faint with hunger, they turned once more, and, not knowing where they were going, stumbled at last upon the street which led to the Antwerp gate.

"I remember this place;" cried Jan, with something like joy in his voice. "Don't you remember, Marie? It's where we stood to watch the soldiers, and Mother sang for us to march, because we were so tired and hungry."

"I'm tired and hungry now, too," said poor Marie.

"Let's march again," said Jan.

"Where to?" said Marie.

"That's the way Father went when he marched away with the soldiers," said Jan, pointing to the Antwerp gate. "Anything is better than staying here. Let's go that way." He started bravely forward once more, Marie and Fidel following.

They found themselves only two wretched atoms in one of the saddest processions in history, for there were many other people, as unhappy as themselves, who were also trying to escape from the city. Some had lived in the section which was now burning; others had been turned out of their homes by the Germans; and all were hastening along, carrying babies and bundles, and followed by groups of older children.

Jan and Marie were swept along with the hurrying crowd, through the city gate and beyond, along the river road which led to Antwerp. No one spoke to them. Doubtless they were supposed to belong to some one of the fleeing families, and it was at least comforting to the children to be near people of whom they were not afraid. But Jan and Marie could not keep pace with the swift-moving crowd of refugees. They trudged along the highway at their best speed, only to find themselves straggling farther and farther behind.

They were half a mile or more beyond the city gate when they overtook a queer little old woman who was plodding steadily along wheeling a wheelbarrow, in front of her. She evidently did not belong among the refugees, for she was making no effort to keep up with them. She had bright, twinkling black eyes, and snow-white hair tucked under a snow-white cap. Her face was as brown as a nut and full of wrinkles, but it shone with such kindness and good-will that, when Jan and Marie had taken one look at her, they could not help walking along by her side.

"Maybe she has seen Mother," whispered Marie to Jan. "Let's ask her!"

The little old woman smiled down at them as they joined her. "You'll have to hurry, my dears, or you won't keep up with your folks," she said kindly.

"They aren't our folks," said Jan.

"They aren't?" said the little old woman, stopping short. "Then where are your folks?"

"We haven't any, not just now," said Jan. "You see our father is a soldier, and our mother, oh, have you seen our mother? She's lost!"

The little old woman gave them a quick, pitying glance. "Lost, is she?" she said. "Well, now, I can't just be sure whether I've seen her or not, not knowing what she looks like, but I wouldn't say I haven't. Lots of folks have passed this way. How did she get lost?" She sat down on the edge of the barrow and drew the children to her side. "Come, now," she said, "tell Granny all about it! I've seen more trouble than any one you ever saw in all your life before, and I'm not a mite afraid of it either."

Comforted already, the children poured forth their story.

"You poor little lambs!" she cried, when they had finished, "and you haven't had a bite to eat since yesterday! Mercy on us! You can never find your mother on an empty stomach!" She rose from the wheelbarrow, as she spoke, and trundled it swiftly from the road to the bank of the river, a short distance away. Here, in a sheltered nook, hidden from the highway by a group of willows, she stopped. "We'll camp right here, and I'll get you a dinner fit for a king or a duke, at the very least," she said cheerily. "Look what I have in my wheelbarrow!" She took a basket from the top of it as she spoke.

Fidel was already looking in, with his tail standing straight out behind, his ears pointed forward, and the hairs bristling on the back of his neck. There, on some clean white sand in the bottom of the wheelbarrow, wriggled a fine fat eel!

"Now I know why I didn't sell that eel," cried Granny. "There's always a reason for everything, you see, my darlings."

She seized the eel with a firm, well-sanded hand as she spoke, and before could spell your name backwards, she had skinned and dressed it, and had given the remnants to poor hungry Fidel. "Now, my boy," she said gayly to Jan as she worked, "you get together some twigs and dead leaves, and you, Big Eyes," she added to Marie, "find some stones by the river, and we'll soon have such a stove as you never saw before, and a fire in it, and a bit of fried eel, to fill your hungry stomachs."

Immensely cheered, the children flew on these errands. Then Marie had a bright thought. "We have some potatoes in our bundle," she said.

"Well, now," cried the little old woman, "wouldn't you think they had just followed up that eel on purpose? We'll put them to roast in the ashes. I always carry a pan and a bit of fat and some matches about with me when I take my eels to market," she explained as she whisked these things out of the basket, "and it often happens that I cook myself a bite to eat on my way home, especially if I'm late. You see, I live a long way from here, just across the river from Boom, and I'm getting lazy in my old age. Early every morning I walk to Malines with my barrow full of fine eels, and sell them to the people of the town. That's how I happen to be so rich!"

"Are you rich?" asked Marie wonderingly.

She had brought the stones from the river, and now she untied her bundle and took out the potatoes. Jan had already heaped a little mound of sticks and twigs near by, and soon the potatoes were cooking in the ashes, and a most appetizing smell of frying eel filled the air.

"Am I rich?" repeated the old woman. She looked surprised that any one could ask such a question. "Of course I'm rich. Haven't I got two eyes in my head, and a tongue, too, and it's lucky, indeed, that it's that way about, for if I had but one eye and two tongues, you see for yourself how much less handy that would be! And I've two legs as good as any one's, and two hands to help myself with! The Kaiser himself has no more legs and arms than I, and I doubt if he can use them half as well. Neither has he a stomach the more! And as for his heart" she looked cautiously around as she spoke "his heart, I'll be bound, is not half so good as mine! If it were, he could not find it in it to do all the cruel things he's doing here. I'm sure of that."

For a moment the cheerfulness of her face clouded over; but she saw the shadow reflected in the faces of Jan and Marie, and at once spoke more gayly. "Bless you, yes, I'm rich," she went on; "and so are you! You've got all the things that I have and more, too, for you legs and arms are young, and you have a mother to look for. Not every one has that, you may depend! And one of these days you'll find her. Make no doubt of that."

"If we don't, she'll surely find us, anyway," said Jan. "She said she would!"

"Indeed and she will," said the old woman. "Even the Germans couldn't stop her; so what matter is it, if you both have to look a bit first? It will only make it the better when you find each other again."

When the potatoes were done, the little old woman raked them out of the ashes with a stick, broke them open, sprinkled a bit of salt on them from the wonderful basket, and then handed one to each of the children, wrapped in a plantain leaf, so they should not burn their fingers. A piece of the eel was served to them in the same way, and Granny beamed with satisfaction as she watched her famished guests.

"Aren't you going to eat, too?" asked Marie with her mouth full.

"Bless you, yes," said Granny. "Every chance I get. You just watch me!" She made a great show of taking a piece of the eel as she spoke, but if any one had been watching carefully, they would have her slyly put it back again into the pan, and the children never knew that they ate her share and their own, too.

When they had eaten every scrap of the eel, and Fidel had finished the bones, the little old woman rose briskly from the bank, washed her pan in the river, packed it in her basket again, and led the way up the path to the highway once more. Although they found the road still filled with the flying refugees, the world had grown suddenly brighter to Jan and Marie. They had found a friend and they were fed.

"Now, you come along home with your Granny," said the little old woman as they reached the Antwerp road and turned northward, "for I live in a little house by the river right on the way to wherever you want to go!"

CHAPTER IX. OFF FOR ANTWERP

For several days the children stayed with the little old woman in her tiny cottage on the edge of the river. Each morning they crossed the bridge and stationed themselves by the Antwerp road to watch the swarm of sad-faced Belgians as they hurried through Boom on their way to the frontier and to safety in Holland. Each day they hoped that before the sun went down they should see their mother among the hurrying multitudes, but each day brought a fresh disappointment, and each night the little old woman comforted them with fresh hope for the morrow.

"You see, my darlings," said she, "it may take a long time and you may have to go a long way first, but I feel in my bones that you will find her at last. And of course, if you do, every step you take is a step toward her, no matter how far round you go."

Jan and Marie believed every word that Granny said. How could they help it when she had been so good to them! Her courage and faith seemed to make an isle of safety about her where the children rested in perfect trust. They saw that neither guns nor Germans nor any other terror could frighten Granny. In the midst of a thousand alarms she calmly went her accustomed way, and every one who met her was the better for a glimpse of the brave little brown face under its snowy cap. Early each morning she rose with the larks, covered the bottom of her barrow with clean white sand, and placed in it the live eels which had been caught for her and brought to the door by small boys who lived in the neighborhood. Then, when she had wakened the Twins, and the three had had their breakfast together, away she would trudge over the long, dusty road to Malines, wheeling the barrow with its squirming freight in front of her.

Jan and Marie helped her all they could. They washed the dishes and swept the floor of the tiny cottage and made everything tidy and clean before they went to take up their stand beside the Antwerp road. When the shadows grew long in the afternoon, how glad they were to see the sturdy little figure come trudging home again! Then they would run to meet her, and Jan would take the wheelbarrow from her tired hands and wheel it for her over the bridge to the little cottage under the willow trees on the other side of the river.

Then Marie's work was to clean the barrow, while Jan pulled weeds in the tiny garden back of the house, and Granny got supper ready. Supper-time was the best of all, for every pleasant evening they ate at a little table out of doors under the willow trees.

One evening, when supper had been cleared away, they sat there together, with Fidel beside them, while Granny told a wonderful tale about the King of the Eels who lived in a crystal palace at the bottom of the river.

"You can't quite see the palace," she said, "because, when you look right down into it, the water seems muddy. But sometimes, when it is still, you can see the Upside-Down Country where the King of the Eels lives. There the trees all grow with their heads down and the sky is 'way, 'way below the trees. You see the sky might as well be down as up for the eels. They aren't like us, just obliged to crawl around on the ground without ever being able to go up or down at all. The up-above sky belongs to the birds and the down-below sky belongs to the fishes and eels. And I am not sure but one is just as nice as the other."

Marie and Jan went to the river, and, getting down on their hands and knees, looked into the water.

"We can't see a thing!" they cried to Granny.

"You aren't looking the right way," she answered. "Look across it toward the sunset."

"Oh! Oh!" cried Marie, clasping her hands; "I see it! I see the down-below sky, and it is all red and gold!"

"I told you so," replied Granny triumphantly. "Lots of folks can't see a thing in the river but the mud, when, if you look at it the right way, there is a whole lovely world in it. Now, the palace of the King of the Eels is right over in that direction where the color is the reddest. He is very fond of red, is the King of the Eels. His throne is all made of rubies, and he makes the Queen tie red bows on the tails of all the little eels."

Jan and Marie were still looking with all their eyes across the still water toward the sunset and trying to see the crystal palace of the eels, when suddenly from behind them there came a loud "Hee-haw, hee-haw." They jumped, and Granny jumped, too, and they all looked around to see where the sound came from.

There, coming slowly toward them along the tow-path on the river-bank, was an old brown mule. She was pulling a low, green river-boat by a towline, and a small boy, not much bigger than Jan, was driving her. On the deck of the boat there was a little cabin with white curtains in the tiny windows and two red geraniums in pots standing on the sills. From a clothesline hitched to the rigging there fluttered a row of little shirts, and seated on a box near by there was a fat, friendly looking woman with two small children playing by her side. The father of the family was busy with the tiller.

"There come the De Smets, as sure as you live!" cried Granny, rising from the wheelbarrow, where she had been sitting. "I certainly am glad to see them." And she started at once down the river to meet the boat, with Jan and Marie and Fidel all following.

"Ship ahoy!" she cried gayly as the boat drew near. The boy who was driving the mule grinned shyly. The woman on deck lifted her eyes from her sewing, smiled, and waved her hand at Granny, while the two little children ran to the edge of the boat; and held out their arms to her.

"Here we are again, war or no war!" cried Mother De Smet, as the boat came alongside. Father De Smet left the tiller and threw a rope ashore. "Whoa!" cried the boy driving the mule. The mule stopped with the greatest willingness, the boy caught the rope and lifted the great loop over a strong post on the river-bank, and the "Old Woman" for that was the name of the boat was in port.

Soon a gangplank was slipped from the boat to the little wooden steps on the bank, and Mother De Smet, with a squirming baby under each arm, came ashore. "I do like to get out on dry land and shake my legs a bit now and then," she said cheerfully as she greeted Granny. "On the boat I just sit still and grow fat!"

"I shake my legs for a matter of ten miles every day," laughed Granny. "That's how I keep my figure!"

Mother De Smet set the babies down on the grass, where they immediately began to tumble about like a pair of puppies, and she and Granny talked together, while the Twins went to watch the work of Father De Smet and the boy, whose name was Joseph.

"I don't know whatever the country is coming to," said Mother De Smet to Granny. "The Germans are everywhere, and they are taking everything that they can lay their hands on. I doubt if we ever get our cargo safe to Antwerp this time. We've come for a load of potatoes, but I am very much afraid it is going to be our last trip for some time. The country looks quiet enough as you see it from the boat, but the things that are happening in it would chill your blood."

"Yes," sighed Granny; "if I would let it, my old heart would break over the sights that I see every day on my way to Malines. But a broken heart won't get you anywhere. Maybe a stout heart will."

"Who are the children you have with you?" asked Mother De Smet.

Then Granny told her how she had found Jan and Marie, and all the rest of the sad story. Mother De Smet wiped her eyes and blew her nose very hard as she listened.

"I wouldn't let them wait any longer by the Antwerp road, anyway," she said when Granny had finished. "There is no use in the world in looking for their mother to come that way. She was probably driven over the border long ago. You just leave them with me to-morrow while you go to town. 'Twill cheer them up a bit to play with Joseph and the babies."

"Well, now," said Granny, "if that isn't just like your good heart!"

And that is how it happened that, when she trudged off with her barrow the next morning, the Twins ran down to the boat and spent the day rolling on the grass with the babies, and helping Father De Smet and Joseph to load the boat with bags of potatoes which had been brought to the dock in the night by neighboring farmers.

When Granny came trundling her barrow home in the late afternoon, she found the children and their new friends already on the best of terms; and that night, after the Twins were in bed, she went aboard the "Old Woman" and talked for a long time with Father and Mother De Smet. No one will ever know just what they said to each other, but it must be that they talked about the Twins, for when the children awoke the next morning, they found Granny standing beside their bed with their clothes all nicely washed and ironed in her hands.

"I'm not going to town this morning with my eels," she said as she popped them out of bed. "I'm going to stay at home and see you off on your journey!" She did not tell them that things had grown so terrible in Malines that even she felt it wise to stay away.

"Our journey!" cried the Twins in astonishment. "What journey?"

"To Antwerp," cried Granny. "Now, you never thought a chance like that would come to you, I'm sure, but some people are born lucky! You see the De Smets start back today, and they are willing to take you along with them!"

"But we don't want to leave you, dear, dear Granny!" cried the Twins, throwing their arms about her neck.

"And I don't want you to go, either, my lambs," said Granny; "but, you see, there are lots of things to think of. In the first place, of course you want to go on hunting for your mother. It may be she has gone over the border; for the Germans are already in trenches near Antwerp, and our army is nearer still to Antwerp and in trenches, too. There they stay, Father De Smet says, for all the world, like two tigers, lying ready to spring at each other's throats. He says Antwerp is so strongly fortified that the Germans can never take it, and so it is a better place to be in than here. The De Smets will see that you are left in safe hands, and I'm sure your mother would want you to go."

The children considered this for a moment in silence.

At last Jan said, "Do you think Father De Smet would let me help drive the mule?"

"I haven't a doubt of it," said Granny.

"But what about Fidel, our dear Fidel?" cried Marie.

"I tell you what I'll do;" said Granny. "I'll take care of Fidel for you! You shall leave him here with me until you come back again! You see, I really need good company, and since I can't have you, I know you would be glad to have Fidel stay here to protect me. Then you'll always know just where he is."

She hurried the children into their clothes as she talked, gave them a good breakfast, and before they had time to think much about what was happening to them, they had said good-bye to Fidel, who had to be shut in the cottage to keep him from following the boat, and were safely aboard the "Old Woman" and slowly moving away down the river. They stood in the stern of the boat, listening to Fidel's wild barks, and waving their hands, until Granny's kind face was a mere round speck in the distance.

CHAPTER X. ON THE TOW-PATH

When they could no longer see Granny, nor hear Fidel, the children sat down on a coil of rope behind the cabin and felt very miserable indeed. Marie was just turning up the corner of her apron to wipe her eyes, and Jan was looking at nothing at all and winking very hard, when good Mother De Smet, came by with a baby waddling along on each side of her. She gave the two dismal little faces a quick glance and then said kindly:

"Jan, you run and see if you can't help Father with the tiller, and, Marie, would you mind playing with the babies while I put on the soup-kettle and fix the greens for dinner? They are beginning to climb everywhere now, and I am afraid they will fall overboard if somebody doesn't watch them every minute!"

Jan clattered at once across the deck to Father De Smet, and Marie gladly followed his wife to the open space in front of the cabin where the babies had room to roll about. Half an hour later, when Mother De Smet went back to get some potatoes for the soup, she found Jan proudly steering the boat by himself.

"Oh, my soul!" she cried in astonishment. "What a clever boy you must be to learn so quickly to handle the tiller. Where is Father De Smet?"

"Here!" boomed a loud voice behind her, and Father De Smet's head appeared above a barrel on the other side of the deck. "I'm trying to make the 'Old Woman' look as if she had no cargo aboard. If the Germans see these potatoes, they'll never let us get them to Antwerp," he shouted.

"Sh-h-h! You mustn't talk so loud," whispered Mother De Smet. "You roar like a foghorn on a dark night. The Germans won't have any trouble in finding out about the potatoes if you shout the news all over the landscape."

Father De Smet looked out over the quiet Belgian fields.

"There's nobody about that I can see," he said, "but I'll roar more gently next time."

There was a bend in the river just at this point, and Jan, looking fearfully about to see if he could see any Germans, for an instant forgot all about the tiller. There was a jerk on the tow-rope and a bump as the nose of the "Old Woman" ran into the river-bank. Netteke, the mule, came to a sudden stop, and Mother De Smet sat down equally suddenly on a coil of rope. Her potatoes spilled over the deck, while a wail from the front of the boat announced that one of the babies had bumped, too. Mother De Smet picked herself up and ran to see what was the matter with the baby, while Father De Smet seized a long pole and hurried forward. Joseph left the mule to browse upon the grass beside the tow-path and ran back to the boat. His father threw him a pole which was kept for such emergencies, and they both pushed. Joseph pushed on the boat and his father pushed against the river-bank. Meanwhile poor Jan stood wretchedly by the tiller knowing that his carelessness had caused the trouble, yet not knowing what to do to help.

"Never mind, son," said Mother De Smet kindly, when she came back for her potatoes and saw his downcast face. "It isn't the first time the 'Old Woman' has stuck her nose in the mud, and with older people than you at the tiller, too! We'll soon have her off again and no harm done."

The boat gave a little lurch toward the middle of the stream.

"Look alive there, Mate!" sang out Father De Smet. "Hard aport with the tiller! Head her out into the stream!"

Joseph flung his pole to his father and rushed back to Netteke, pulled her patient nose out of a delicious bunch of thistles and started her up the tow-path. Jan sprang to the tiller, and soon the "Old Woman" was once more gliding smoothly over the quiet water toward Antwerp.

When Father De Smet came back to the stern of the boat, Jan expected a scolding, but perhaps it seemed to the good-natured skipper that Jan had troubles enough already, for he only said mildly, "Stick to your job, son, whatever it is," and went on covering his potatoes with empty boxes and pieces of sailcloth. Jan paid such strict attention to the tiller after that that he did not even forget when Father De Smet pointed out a burning farmhouse a mile or so from the river and said grimly, "The Germans are amusing themselves again."

For the most part, however, the countryside seemed so quiet and peaceful that it was hard to believe that such dreadful things were going on all about them. While Father De Smet's eyes, under their bushy brows, kept close watch in every direction, he said little about his fears and went on his way exactly as he had done before the invasion.

It was quite early in the morning when they left Boom, and by ten o'clock Joseph was tired of trudging along beside Netteke. He hailed his father.

"May I come aboard now?" he shouted.

Father De Smet looked at Jan.

"Would you like to drive the mule awhile?" he asked.

"Oh, wouldn't I!" cried Jan.

"Have you ever driven a mule before?" Father De Smet asked again.

"Not a mule, exactly," Jail replied, "but I drove old Pier up from the field with a load of wheat all by myself. Mother sat on the load."

"Come along!" shouted Father De Smet to Joseph, and in a moment the gangplank was out and Jan and Joseph had changed places.

"May I go, too?" asked Marie timidly of Father De Smet as he was about to draw in the plank. "The babies are both asleep and I have nothing to do."

Father De Smet took a careful look in every direction. It was level, open country all about them, dotted here and there with farmhouses, and in the distance the spire of a village church rose above the clustering houses and pointed to the sky.

"Yes, yes, child. Go ahead," said Father De Smet. "Only don't get too near Netteke's hind legs. She doesn't know you very well and sometimes she forgets her manners."

Marie skipped over the gangplank and ran along the tow-path to Jan, who already had taken up Netteke's reins and was waiting for the signal to start. Joseph took his place at the tiller, and again the "Old Woman" moved slowly down the stream.

For some time Jan and Marie plodded along with Netteke. At first they thought it good fun, but by and by, as the sun grew hot, driving a mule on a tow-path did not seem quite so pleasant a task as they had thought it would be.

"I'm tired of this," said Jan at last to Marie. "That mule is so slow that I have to sight her by something to be sure that she is moving at all! I've been measuring by that farmhouse across the river for a long time, and she hasn't crawled up to it yet! I shouldn't wonder if she'd go to sleep some day and fall into the river and never wake up! Why, I am almost asleep myself."

"She'll wake up fast enough when it's time to eat, and so will you," said Marie, with profound wisdom.

"Let 's see if we can't make her go a little faster, anyway," said Jan, ignoring Marie's remark. "I know what I'll do," he went on, chuckling; "I'll get some burrs and stick them in her tail, and then every time she slaps the flies off she'll make herself go faster."

Marie seized Jan's arm.

"You'll do nothing of the kind!" she cried. "Father De Smet told me especially to keep away from Netteke's hind legs."

"Pooh!" said Jan; "he didn't tell me that. I'm not afraid of any mule alive. I guess if I can harness a horse and drive home a load of grain from the field, there isn't much I can't do with a mule!" To prove his words he shouted "U - U" at Netteke and slapped her flank with a long branch of willow.

Now, Netteke was a proud mule and she wasn't used to being slapped. Father De Smet knew her ways, and knew also that her steady, even, slow pace was better in the long run than to attempt to force a livelier gait, and Netteke was well aware of what was expected of her. She resented being interfered with. Instead of going forward at greater speed, she put her four feet together, laid back her ears, gave a loud "hee-haw!" and stopped stock-still.

"U - U!" shouted Jan. In vain! Netteke would not move. Marie held a handful of fresh grass just out of reach of her mouth. But Netteke was really offended. She made no effort to get it. She simply stayed where she was. Father De Smet stuck his head over the side of the boat.

"What is the matter?" he shouted.

"Oh, dear!" said Jan to Marie. "I hoped he wouldn't notice that the boat wasn't moving."

"Netteke has stopped. She won't go at all. I think she's run down!" Marie called back.

"Try coaxing her," cried the skipper. "Give her something to eat. Hold it in front of her nose."

"I have," answered Marie, "but she won't even look at it."

"Then it's no use," said Father De Smet mournfully. "She's balked and that is all there is to it. We'll just have to wait until she is ready to go again. When she has made up her mind she is as difficult to persuade as a setting hen."

Mother De Smet's head appeared beside her husband's over the boat-rail.

"Oh, dear!" said she; "I hoped we should get to the other side of the line before dark, but if Netteke's set, she's set, and we must just make the best of it. It's lucky it's dinner-time. We'll eat, and maybe by the time we are through she'll be willing to start." Father De Smet tossed a bucket on to the grass.

"Give her a good drink," he said, "and come aboard yourselves."

Jan filled the bucket from the river and set it down before Netteke, but she was in no mood for blandishments. She kept her ears back and would not touch the water.

"All right, then, Crosspatch," said Jan. Leaving the pail in front of her, he went back to the boat. The gangplank was put out, and he and Marie went on board.

They found dinner ready in the tiny cabin, and because it was so small and stuffy, and there were too many of them, anyway, to get into it comfortably, they each took a bowl of soup as Mother De Smet handed it to them and sat down on the deck in front of the cabin to eat it. It was not until the middle of the afternoon that Netteke forgot her injuries, consented to eat and drink, and indicated her willingness to move on toward Antwerp.

CHAPTER XI. THE ATTACK

Joseph and his father were both on the tow-path when at last Netteke decided to move. As she set her ears forward and took the first step, Father De Smet heaved a sigh of relief.

"Now, why couldn't you have done that long ago, you addlepated old fool," he said mildly to Netteke. "You have made no end of trouble for us, and gained nothing for yourself! Now I am afraid we shan't get beyond the German lines before dark. We may even have to spend the night in dangerous territory, and all because you're just as mulish as, as a mule," he finished helplessly.

Joseph laughed. "Can't you think of anything mulisher than a mule?" he said.

"There isn't a thing," answered his father.

"Well," answered Joseph, "there are a whole lot of other things beside balky mules in this world that I wish had never been made. There are spiders, and rats, and Germans. They are all pests. I don't see why they were ever born."

Father De Smet became serious at once.

"Son," he said sternly, "don't ever let me hear you say such a thing again. There are spiders, and rats, and balky mules, and Germans, and it doesn't do a bit of good to waste words fussing because they are here. The thing to do is to deal with them!"

Father De Smet was so much in earnest that he boomed these words out in quite a loud voice. Joseph seized his hand.

"Hush!" he whispered.

Father De Smet looked up. There, standing right in front of them in the tow-path, was a German soldier!

"Halt!" shouted the soldier.

But Netteke was now just as much bent upon going as she had been before upon standing still. She paid no attention whatever to the command, but walked stolidly along the tow-path directly toward the soldier.

"Halt!" cried the soldier again.

But Netteke had had no military training, and she simply kept on. In one more step she would have come down upon the soldier's toes, if he had not moved aside just in time. He was very angry.

"Why didn't you stop your miserable old mule when I told you to?" he said to Father De Smet.

"It's a balky mule," replied Father De Smet mildly, "and very obstinate."

"Indeed!" sneered the soldier; "then, I suppose you have named him Albert after your pig-headed King!"

"No," answered Father De Smet, "I think too much of my King to name my mule after him."

"Oh, ho!" said the German; "then perhaps you have named him for the Kaiser!"

Netteke had marched steadily along during this conversation, and they were now past the soldier.

"No," Father De Smet called back, "I didn't name her after the Kaiser. I think too much of my mule!"

The soldier shook his fist after them. "I'll make you pay well for your impudence!" he shouted. "You and I will meet again!"

"Very likely," muttered Father De Smet under his breath. He was now more than ever anxious to get beyond the German lines before dark, but as the afternoon passed it became certain that they would not be able to do it. The shadows grew longer and longer as Netteke plodded slowly along, and at last Mother De Smet called to her husband over the boatside.

"I think we shall have to stop soon and feed the mule or she will be too tired to get us across the line at all. I believe we should save time by stopping for supper. Besides, I want to send over there," she pointed to a farmhouse not a great distance from the river, "and get some milk and eggs."

"Very well," said her husband; "we'll stop under that bunch of willows."

The bunch of willows beside the river which he pointed out proved to be a pleasant, sheltered spot, with grassy banks sloping down to the water. A turn in the river enabled them to draw the "Old Woman" up into their shadows, and because the trees were green and the boat was green, the reflections in the water were also green, and for this reason the boat seemed very well hidden from view.

"I don't believe we shall be noticed here," said Father De Smet.

"It's hot on the boat. It would be nice to take the babies ashore while we eat," said Mother De Smet, running out the gangplank. "I believe we'll have supper on the grass. You hurry along and get the milk and eggs, and I'll cook some onions while you are gone."

Jan and Marie ran over the plank at once, and Mother De Smet soon followed with the babies. Then, while Marie watched them, she and Jan brought out the onions and a pan, and soon the air was heavy with the smell of frying onions. Joseph and Jan slipped the bridle over Netteke's collar and allowed her to eat the rich green grass at the river's edge. When Father De Smet returned, supper was nearly ready. He sniffed appreciatively as he appeared under the trees.

"Smells good," he said as he held out the milk and eggs toward his wife.

"Sie haben recht!" (You are right!), said a loud voice right behind him!

Father De Smet was so startled that he dropped the eggs. He whirled about, and there stood the German soldier who had told Netteke to halt. With him were six other men.

"Ha! I told you we should meet again!" shouted the soldier to Father De Smet. "And it was certainly thoughtful of you to provide for our entertainment. Comrades, fall to!"

The onions were still cooking over a little blaze of twigs aid dry leaves, but Mother De Smet was no longer tending them. The instant she heard the gruff voice she had dropped her spoon, and, seizing a baby under each arm, had fled up the gangplank on to the boat. Marie followed at top speed. Father De Smet faced the intruders.

"What do you want here?" he said.

"Some supper first," said the soldier gayly, helping himself to some onions and passing the pan to his friends. "Then, perhaps, a few supplies for our brave army. There is no hurry. After supper will do; but first we'll drink a health to the Kaiser, and since you are host here, you shall propose it!"

He pointed to the pail of milk which Father De Smet still held.

"Now," he shouted, "lift your stein and say, 'Hoch der Kaiser.'"

Father De Smet looked them in the face and said not a word. Meanwhile Jan and Joseph, to Mother De Smet's great alarm, had not followed her, on to the boat. Instead they had flown to Netteke, who was partly hidden from the group by a bunch of young willows near the water's edge, and with great speed and presence of mind had slipped her bridle over her head and gently started her up the tow-path.

"Oh," murmured Joseph, "suppose she should balk!" But Netteke had done her balking for the day, and, having been refreshed by her luncheon of green grass, she was ready to move on. The river had now quite a current, which helped them, and while the soldiers were still having their joke with Father De Smet the boat moved quietly out of sight. As she felt it move, Mother De Smet lifted her head over the boat's rail behind which she and the children were hiding, and raised the end of the gangplank so that it would make no noise by scraping along the ground. She was beside herself with anxiety. If she screamed or said anything to the boys, the attention of the soldiers would immediately be directed toward them. Yet if they should by any miracle succeed in getting away, there was her husband left alone to face seven enemies. She wrung her hands.

"Maybe they will stop to eat the onions," she groaned to herself. She held to the gangplank and murmured prayers to all the saints she knew, while Jan and Joseph trotted briskly along the tow-path, and Netteke, assisted by the current, made better speed than she had at any time during the day.

Meanwhile his captors were busy with Father De Smet. "Come! Drink to the Kaiser!" shouted the first soldier, "or we'll feed you to the fishes! We want our supper, and you delay us." Still Father De Smet said nothing. "We'll give you just until I count ten," said the soldier, pointing his gun at him, "and if by that time you have not found your tongue -"

But he did not finish the sentence. From an unexpected quarter a shot rang out. It struck the pail of milk and dashed it over the German and over Father De Smet too. Another shot followed, and the right arm of the soldier fell helpless to his side. One of his companions gave a howl and fell to the ground. Still no one appeared at whom the Germans could direct their fire. "Snipers!" shouted the soldiers, instantly lowering their guns, but before they could even fire in the direction of the unseen enemy, there was such a patter of bullets about them that they turned and fled.

Father De Smet fled, too. He leaped over the frying-pan and tore down the river-bank after the boat. As he overtook it, Mother De Smet ran out the gang plank. "Boys!" shouted Father De Smet. "Get aboard! Get aboard!" Joseph and Jan instantly stopped the mule and, dropping the reins, raced up the gangplank, almost before the end of it rested safely on the ground. Father De Smet snatched up the reins. On went the boat at Netteke's best speed, which seemed no better than a snail's pace to the fleeing family. Sounds of the skirmish continued to reach their ears, even when they had gone some distance down the river, and it was not until twilight had deepened into dusk, and they were hidden in its shadows, that they dared hope the danger was passed. It was after ten o'clock at night when the "Old Woman" at last approached the twinkling lights of Antwerp, and they knew that, for the time being at least, they were safe.

They wore now beyond the German lines in country still held by the Belgians. Here, in a suburb of the city, Father De Smet decided to dock for the night. A distant clock struck eleven as the hungry but thankful family gathered upon the deck of the "Old Woman" to eat a meager supper of bread and cheese with only the moon to light their repast. Not until they had finished did Father De Smet tell them all that had happened to him during the few terrible moments when he was in the hands of the enemy.

"They overreached themselves," he said. "They meant to amuse themselves by prolonging my misery, and they lingered just a bit too long." He turned to Jan and Joseph. "You were brave boys! If you had not started the boat when you did, it is quite likely they might have got me, after all, and the potatoes too. I am proud of you."

"But, Father," cried Joseph, "who could have fired those shots? We didn't see a soul."

"Neither did I," answered his father; "and neither did the Germans for that matter. There was no one in sight."

"Oh," cried Mother De Smet, "it was as if the good God himself intervened to save you!"

"As I figure it out," said Father De Smet, "we must have stopped very near the trenches, and our own men must have seen the Germans attack us. My German friend had evidently been following us up, meaning to get everything we had and me too. But the smell of the onions was too much for him! If he hadn't been greedy, he might have carried out his plan, but he wanted our potatoes and our supper too; and so he got neither!" he chuckled. "And neither did the Kaiser get a toast from me! Instead, he got a salute from the Belgians." He crossed himself reverently. "Thank God for our soldiers," he said, and Mother De Smet, weeping softly, murmured a devout "Amen."

Little did Jan and Marie dream as they listened, that this blessing rested upon their own father, and that he had been one of the Belgian soldiers, who, firing from the trenches, had delivered them from the hands of their enemies. Their father, hidden away, in the earth like a fox, as little dreamed that he had helped to save his own children from a terrible fate.

CHAPTER XII. THE ZEPPELIN RAID

When the Twins awoke, early the next morning, they found that Father and Mother De Smet had been stirring much earlier still, and that the "Old Woman" was already slipping quietly along among the docks of Antwerp. To their immense surprise they were being towed, not by Netteke, but by a very small and puffy steam tug. They were further astonished to find that Netteke herself was on board the "Old Woman."

"How in the world did you get the mule on to the boat!" gasped Jan, when he saw her.

"Led her right up the gangplank just like folks," answered Father De Smet. "I couldn't leave her behind and I wanted to get to the Antwerp docks as soon as possible. This was the quickest way. You see," he went on, "I don't know where I shall be going next, but I know it won't be up the Dyle, so I am going to keep Netteke right where I can use her any minute."

There was no time for further questions, for Father De Smet had to devote his attention to the tiller. Soon they were safely in dock and Father De Smet was unloading his potatoes and selling them to the market-men, who swarmed about the boats to buy the produce which had been brought in from the country.

"There!" he said with a sigh of relief as he delivered the last of his cargo to a purchaser late in the afternoon; "that load is safe from the Germans, anyway."

"How did you find things up the Dyle?" asked the merchant who had bought the potatoes.

Father De Smet shook his head.

"Couldn't well be worse," he said. "I'm not going to risk another trip. The Germans are taking everything they can lay their hands on, and are destroying what they can't seize. I nearly lost this load, and my life into the bargain. If it hadn't been that, without knowing it, we stopped so near the Belgian line of trenches that they could fire on the German foragers who tried to take our cargo, I shouldn't have been here to tell this tale."

"God only knows what will become of Belgium if this state of things continues," groaned the merchant. "Food must come from somewhere or the people will starve."

"True enough," answered Father De Smet. "I believe I'll try a trip north through the back channels of the Scheldt and see what I can pick up."

"Don't give up, anyway," urged the merchant. "If you fellows go back on us, I don't know what we shall do. We depend on you to bring supplies from somewhere, and if you can't get them in Belgium, you'll have to go up into Holland."

Mother De Smet leaned over the boatrail and spoke to the two men who were standing on the dock.

"You'd better believe we'll not give up," she said. "We don't know the meaning of the word."

"Well," said the merchant sadly, "maybe you don't, but there are others who do. It takes a stout heart to have faith that God hasn't forgotten Belgium these days."

"It's easy enough to have faith when things are going right," said Mother De Smet, "but to have faith when things are going wrong isn't so easy." Then she remembered Granny. "But a sick heart won't get you anywhere, and maybe a stout one will," she finished.

"That's a good word," said the merchant.

"It was said by as good a woman as treads shoe-leather," answered Mother De Smet.

"You are safe while you stay in Antwerp, anyway," said the merchant as he turned to say good-bye. "Our forts are the strongest in the world and the Germans will never be able to take them. There's comfort in that for us." Then he spoke to his horses and turned away with his load.

"Let us stay right here to-night," said Mother De Smet to her husband as he came on board the boat. "We are all in need of rest after yesterday, and in

Antwerp we can get a good night's sleep. Besides, it is so late in the day that we couldn't get out of town before dark if we tried."

Following this plan, the whole family went to bed at dusk, but they were not destined to enjoy the quiet sleep they longed for. The night was warm, and the cabin small, so Father De Smet and Joseph, as well as the Twins, spread bedding on the deck and went to sleep looking up at the stars.

They had slept for some hours when they were suddenly aroused by the sound of a terrific explosion. Instantly they sprang to their feet, wide awake, and Mother De Smet came rushing from the cabin with the babies screaming in her arms.

"What is it now? What is it?" she cried.

"Look! Look!" cried Jan.

He pointed to the sky. There, blazing with light, like a great misshapen moon, was a giant airship moving swiftly over the city. As it sailed along, streams of fire fell from it, and immediately there followed the terrible thunder of bursting bombs. When it passed out of sight, it seemed as if the voice of the city itself must rise in anguish at the terrible destruction left in its wake.

Just what that destruction was, Father De Smet did not wish to see. "This is a good place to get away from," he said to the frightened group cowering on the deck of the "Old Woman" after the bright terror had disappeared. When morning came he lost no time in making the best speed he could away from the doomed city of Antwerp which they had thought so safe.

When they had left the city behind them and the boat was slowly making its way through the quiet back channels of the Scheldt the world once more seemed really peaceful to the wandering children. Their way lay over still waters and beside green pastures, and as they had no communication with the stricken regions of Belgium, they had no news of the progress of the war, until, some days later, the boat docked at Rotterdam, and it became necessary to decide what should be done next. There they learned that they had barely escaped the siege of Antwerp, which had begun with the Zeppelin raid.

Father De Smet was now obliged to confront the problem of what to do with his own family, for, since Antwerp was now in the hands of the enemy, he could no longer earn his living in the old way. Under these changed conditions he could not take care of Jan and Marie, so one sad day they said good-bye to good Mother De Smet, to Joseph and the babies, and went with Father De Smet into the city of Rotterdam.

They found that these streets were also full of Belgian refugees, and here, too, they watched for their mother. In order to keep up her courage, Marie had often to feel of the locket and to say to herself: "She will find us. She will find us." And Jan, Jan had many times to say to himself, "I am now a man and must be brave," or he would have cried in despair.

But help was nearer than they supposed. Already England had begun to organize for the relief of the Belgian refugees, and it was in the office of the British Consul at Rotterdam that Father De Smet finally took leave of Jan and Marie. The Consul took them that night to his own home, and, after a careful record had been made of their names and their parents' names and all the facts about them, they were next day placed upon a ship, in company with many other homeless Belgians, and sent across the North Sea to England.

CHAPTER XIII. REFUGEES

If I were to tell you all the strange new sights that Jan and Marie saw, and all the things they did in England, it would make this book so big you could not hold it up to read it, so I must skip all about the great house in the southern part of England where they next found themselves. This house was the great country place of a very rich man, and when the war broke out he had given it to be used as a shelter for homeless Belgians. There were the most wonderful woods and parks on the estate, and miles of beautiful drives. There were great gardens and stables and hothouses; and the house was much bigger and finer than any Jan and Marie had ever seen in all their lives. It seemed to them as if they had suddenly been changed into a prince and princess by some fairy wand. They were not alone in all this splendor; other lost little Belgian children were there, and there were lost parents, too, and it seemed such a pity that the lost parents and the lost children should not be the very ones that belonged together, so that every one could be happy once more. However, bad as it was, it was so much better than anything they had known since the dreadful first night of the alarm that Jan and Marie became almost happy again.

At night they and the other homeless children slept in little white cots set all in a row in a great picture gallery. They were given new clothes, for by this time even their best ones were quite worn out, and every day they had plenty of good plain food to eat. Every day more Belgians came, and still more, until not only the big house, but the stable and outbuildings were all running-over full of homeless people.

One day, after they had been in this place for two or three weeks, Jan and Marie were called into the room where sat the sweet-faced lady whose home they were in. It was like an office, and there were several other persons there with her.

The sweet-faced lady spoke to them. "Jan and Marie," she said, "how would you like to go to live with a dear lady in America who would love you, and take care of you, so you need never be lonely and sad again?"

"But our mother!" gasped Marie, bursting into tears. "We have not found her!"

"You will not lose her any more by going to America," said the lady, "for, you see, we shall know all about you here, and if your mother comes, we shall be able to tell her just where to find you. Meanwhile you will be safe and well cared for, far away from all the dreadful things that are happening here."

"It is so far away!" sobbed Marie.

Jan said nothing; he was busy swallowing lumps in his own throat.

"You see, dears," the lady said gently, "you can be together there, for this woman has no children of her own, and is willing to take both of you. That does not often happen, and, besides, she is a Belgian; I know you will find a good home with her."

"You're sure we could be together?" asked Jan.

"Yes," said the lady.

"Because," said Jan, "Mother said I must take care of Marie."

"And she said she'd find us again if she had to swim the sea," said Marie, feeling of her locket and smiling through her tears.

"She won't have to swim," said the lady. "We will see to that! If she comes here, she shall go for you in a fine big ship, and so that's all settled." She kissed their woebegone little faces. "You are going to start to-morrow," she said. "The good captain of the ship has promised to take care of you, so you will not be afraid, and I know you will be good children."

It seemed like a month to Jan and Marie, but it was really only seven days later that they stood on the deck of the good ship Caspian, as it steamed proudly into the wonderful harbor of New York. It was dusk, and already the lights of the city sparkled like a sky full of stars dropped down to earth. High above the other stars shone the great torch of "Liberty enlightening the World." "Oh," gasped Marie, as she gazed, "New York must be as big as heaven. Do you suppose that is an angel holding a candle to light us in?"

Just then the captain came to find them, and a few minutes later they walked with him down the gangplank, right into a pair of outstretched arms. The arms belonged to Madame Dujardin, their new mother. "I should have known them the moment I looked at them, even if they hadn't been with the captain," she cried to her husband, who stood smiling by her side. "Poor darlings, your troubles are all over now! Just as soon as Captain Nichols says you may, you shall come with us, and oh, I have so many things to show you in your new home!"

She drew them with her to a quieter part of the dock, while her husband talked with the captain, and then, when they had bidden him good-bye, they were bundled into a waiting motor car and whirled away through miles of brilliantly lighted streets and over a wonderful bridge, and on and on, until they came to green lawns, and houses set among trees and shrubs, and it seemed to the children as if they must have reached the very end of the world. At last the car stopped before a house standing some distance back from the street in a large yard, and the children followed their new friends through the bright doorway of their house.

Madame Dujardin helped them take off their things in the pleasant hallway, where an open fire was burning, and later, when they were washed and ready, she led the way to a cheerful dining room, where there was a pretty table set for four. There were flowers on the table, and they had chicken for supper, and, after that, ice cream! Jan and Marie had never tasted ice cream before in their whole lives! They thought they should like America very much.

After supper their new mother took them upstairs and showed them two little rooms with a bathroom between. One room was all pink and white with a dear little white bed in it, and she said to Marie, "This is your room, my dear." The other room was all in blue and white with another dear little white bed in it, and she said to Jan, "This is your room, my dear." And there were clean white night-gowns on the beds, and little wrappers with gay flowered slippers, just waiting for Jan and Marie to put them on.

"Oh, I believe it is heaven!" cried Marie, as she looked about the pretty room. Then she touched Madame Dujardin's sleeve timidly. "Is it all true?" she said. "Shan't we wake up and have to go somewhere else pretty soon?"

"No, dear," said Madame Dujardin gently. "You are going to stay right here now and be happy."

"It will be a very nice place for Mother to find us in," said Jan. "She will come pretty soon now, I should think."

"I hope she may," said Madame Dujardin, tears twinkling in her eyes.

"I'm sure she will," said Marie. "You see everybody is looking for her. There's Granny, and Mother and Father De Smet, and Joseph, and the people in Rotterdam, and the people in England, too; and then, besides, Mother is looking for herself, of course!"

"She said she would surely find us even if she had to swim the sea," added Jan.

CHAPTER XIV. THE MOST WONDERFUL PART

And now comes the most wonderful part of the story!

Madame Dujardin prepared a bath and said to Marie: "You may have the first turn in the tub because you're a girl. In America the girls have the best of everything", she laughed at Jan, as she spoke. "I will help you undress. Jan, you may get ready and wait for your turn in your own room." She unbuttoned Marie's dress, slipped off her clothes, and held up the gay little wrapper for her to put her arms into, and just then she noticed the locket on her neck. "We'll take this off, too," she said, beginning to unclasp it.

But Marie clung to it with both hands. "No, no," she cried. "Mother said I was never, never to take it off. It has her picture in it."

"May I see it, dear?" asked Madame Dujardin. "I should like to know what your mother looks like." Marie nestled close to her, and Madame Dujardin opened the locket.

For a moment she gazed at the picture in complete silence, her eyes staring at it like two blue lights. Then she burst into a wild fit of weeping, and cried out, "Leonie! Leonie! It is not possible! My own sister's children!" She clasped the bewildered Marie in her arms and kissed her over and over again. She ran to the door and brought in Jan and kissed him; and then she called her husband. When he came in and saw her with her arms around both children at once, holding the locket in her hands, and laughing and crying both together, he, too, was bewildered.

"What in the world is the matter, Julie?" he cried.

For answer, she pointed to the face in the locket. "Leonie! Leonie!" she cried. "They are my own sister's children! Surely the hand of God is in this!"

Her husband looked at the locket. "So it is! So it is!" he said in astonishment. "I thought at first you had gone crazy."

"See!" cried his wife. "It's her wedding-gown, and afterward she gave me those very beads she has around her neck! I have them yet!" She rushed from the room and returned in a moment with the beads in her hand.

Meanwhile Jan and Marie had stood still, too astonished to do more than stare from one amazed and excited face to the other, as their new father and mother gazed, first at them, and then at the locket, and last at the beads, scarcely daring to believe the testimony of their own eyes. "To think," cried Madame Dujardin at last, "that I should not have known! But there are many Van Hoves in Belgium, and it never occurred to me that they could be my own flesh and blood. It is years since I have heard from Leonie. In fact, I hardly knew she had any children, our lives have been so different. Oh, it is all my fault," she cried, weeping again. "But if I have neglected her, I will make it up to her children! It may be, oh, it is just possible that she is still alive, and that she may yet write to me after all these years! Sorrow sometimes bridges wide streams!"

Then she turned more quietly to the children.

"You see, dears," she said, "I left Belgium many years ago, and came with your uncle to this country. We were poor when we came, but your uncle has prospered as one can in America. At first Leonie and I wrote regularly to each other. Then she grew more and more busy, and we seemed to have no ties in common, so that at last we lost sight of each other altogether." She opened her arms to Marie and Jan as she spoke, and held them for some time in a close embrace.

Finally she lifted her head and laughed. "This will never do!" she exclaimed. "You must have your baths, even if you are my own dear niece and nephew. The water must be perfectly cold by this time!"

She went into the bathroom, turned on more hot water, and popped Marie into the tub. In half an hour both children had said their prayers and were tucked away for the night in their clean white beds.

Wonderful days followed for Jan and Marie. They began to go to school; they had pretty clothes and many toys, and began to make friends among the little American children of the neighborhood. But in the midst of these new joys they did not forget their mother, still looking for them, or their father, now fighting, as they supposed, in the cruel trenches of Belgium. But at last there came a day when Aunt Julie received a letter with a foreign postmark. She opened it, with trembling fingers, and when she saw that it began, "My dear Sister Julie," she wept so for joy that she could not see to read it, and her husband had to read it for her.

This was the letter:

You will perhaps wonder at hearing from me after the long years of silence that have passed, but I have never doubted the goodness of your heart, my Julie, nor your love for your poor Leonie, even though our paths in life have led such different ways. And now I must tell you of the sorrows which have broken my heart. Georges was obliged to go into the army at a moment's notice when the war broke out. A few days later the Germans swept through Meer, driving the people before them like chaff before the wind. As our house was on the edge of the village, I was the first to see them coming. I hid the children in the vegetable cellar, but before I could get to a hiding-place for myself, they swept over the town, driving every man, woman, and child before them. To turn back then was impossible, and it was only after weeks of hardship and danger that I at last succeeded in struggling through the territory occupied by Germans to the empty city of Malines, and the deserted village where we had been so happy! On the kitchen door of our home I found a paper pinned. On it was printed, "Dear Mother - We have gone to Malines to find you - Jan and Marie." Since then I have searched every place where there seemed any possibility of my finding my dear children, but no trace of them can I find. Then, through friends in Antwerp, I learned that Georges had been wounded and was in a hospital there and I went at once to find him. He had lost an arm in the fighting before Antwerp and was removed to Holland after the siege began. Here we have remained since, still hoping God would hear our prayers and give us news of our dear children. It would even be a comfort to know surely of their death, and if I could know that they were alive and well, I think I should die of joy. Georges can fight no more; our home is lost; we are beggars until this war is over and our country once more restored to us. I am now at work in a factory, earning what keeps body and soul together. Georges must soon leave the hospital, then, God knows what may befall us. How I wish we had been wise like you, my Julie, and your Paul, and that we had gone, with you to America years ago! I might then have my children with me in comfort. If you get this letter, write to your heart-broken

LEONIE.

It was not a letter that went back that very day; it was a cablegram, and it said:

Jan and Marie are safe with me. Am sending money with this to the Bank of Holland, for your passage to America. Come at once.   JULIE.

People do not die of joy, or I am sure that Father and Mother Van Hove would never have survived the reading of that message. Instead it put such new strength and energy into their weary souls and bodies that two days later they were on their way to England, and a week later still they stood on the deck of the Arabia as it steamed into New York Harbor. Jan and Marie with Uncle Paul and Aunt Julie met them at the dock, and there are very few meetings, this side of heaven, like the reunion of those six persons on that day.

The story of that first evening together can hardly be told. First. Father and Mother Van Hove listened to Jan and Marie as they told of their wanderings with Fidel, of the little old eel woman, of Father and Mother De Smet, of the attack by Germans and of the friends they found in Holland and in England; and when everybody had cried a good deal about that, Father Van Hove told what had happened to him; then Mother Van Hove told of her long and perilous search for her children; and there were more tears of thankfulness and joy, until it seemed as if their hearts were filled to the brim and running over. But when, last of all, Uncle Paul told of the plans which he and Aunt Julie had made for the family, they found there was room in their hearts for still more joy.

"I have a farm in the country," said Uncle Paul. "It is not very far from New York. There is a good house on it; it is already stocked. I need a farmer to take care of the place for me, and trustworthy help is hard to get here. If you will manage it for me, Brother Georges, I shall have no further anxiety about it, and shall expect to enjoy the fruits of it as I have never yet been able to do. Leonie shall make some of her good butter for our city table, and the children" here he pinched Marie's cheek, now round and rosy once more "the children shall pick berries and help on the farm all summer. In winter they can come back to Uncle Paul and Aunt Julie and go to school here, for they are our children now, as well as yours."

Father Van Hove rose, stretched out his one hand, and, grasping Uncle Paul's, tried to thank him, but his voice failed.

"Don't say a word, old man," said Uncle Paul, clasping Father Van Hove's hand with both of his. "All the world owes a debt to Belgium which it can never pay. Her courage and devotion have saved the rest of us from the miseries she has borne so bravely. If you got your just deserts, you'd get much more than I can ever give you."

In the end it all came about just as Uncle Paul had said, and the Van Hoves are living in comfort and happiness on that farm this very day.

Lucy Fitch Perkins – A Short Biography

One of American literature's almost forgotten names, but in the early 20th Century a wildly popular authoress is Lucy Fitch Perkins, author and illustrator of children's books and originator of the popular Twins series. She was born on 12th July 1865 in Maples, Indiana. Her father, Appleton Howe Fitch, had graduated from Amherst college and spent his professional career working as a teacher and eventually become principle of a school in Chicago. Shortly before his daughter's birth he exchanged teaching for the lumber business and the family relocated to Maples for its forestry. Her mother was Elizabeth Bennett.

Both her parents were Puritan, and ensured that a key value in their children's upbringing was education. Though Lucy and her sisters were home-schooled, their parents made sure that they frequently visited Massachusetts and their ancestral home, approximately twenty-five miles out of Boston, where the girls spent time in school so they might experience social interaction with others their age.

Eventually, in 1879, the family permanently removed to the property in Massachusetts, and the girls spent the remainder of their school years here. Lucy displayed early talent in writing and drawing and when she graduated from high school she chose to attend the art school at the Boston Museum of Fine Arts, where she was a student for three years. After graduating, she found employment illustrating for the Prang Educational Company of Boston, where she stayed for a year before moving on to a teaching post at the Pratt Institute, then only recently established.

During these years she made the first inroads into a career in this field, illustrating a translation of The Goose Girl, a German fairy tale made known as Tale no. 89 in the Brothers Grimm's collections, and A Book of Joys: The Story of a New England Summer, which she both wrote and illustrated.

Lucy spent four years working at the Pratt Institute, continuing her own studies while carrying out her teaching duties. She writes of her time there as "happy", enjoying the combination of working on her own talents, while passing them on to others. Then, in 1881, she married a young architect named Dwight Heald Perkins. They had met years earlier while they were both studying in Boston. Their married home was to be in Evanston, Chicago, where Lucy gave birth to Eleanor Ellis and Lawrence Bradford Perkins. They lived here for several years, Lucy working as an illustrator for various publishers and magazines and Dwight as a teacher at the Massachusetts Institute of Technology. They were both active members of their community, and Lucy writes that they "lived fully in the events and thought currents of the time".

She was forty-eight when she was approached by a publisher friend who, aware and impressed by her talents as both an illustrator, which was her profession, and as a writer, which he knew through correspondence, urged her to write. He was so earnest that she thought of an idea for a children's book the next morning, and she immediately set to work making sketches and preparing the idea for presentation. The publisher came to dinner at their house the next evening and she took the opportunity to show him. He responded "go ahead and write it, and I want it". That book was The Dutch Twins, the first in what became a popular series. Using simple language, vivid imagery, stories of adventure and simple moral issues, the stories gently introduced their readers to other countries and cultures, and some of their basic differences with America. Though she had previously published The Goose Girl and A Book of Joys, there is a shift in emphasis from the illustrations to the writing; previously, the illustrations were the primary focus of the books, whereas now, they merely complimented the vividness of her imagery in writing.

Lucy later wrote of the Twins series that they were borne of two key ideas. The first, of "the necessity for mutual respect and understanding between people of different nationalities" if there was ever to be global peace, she felt particularly resonated in her own country, where "all the nations of the earth are represented in the population" (indeed, the term 'melting pot' which we use to describe civilisations where several different cultures are to be found living together was just being coined as a descriptive term in America). The second of these two ideas was that it was possible to hold a child's attention, even when writing about big, complex ideas, so long as the language and story were engaging. As an example, in The Dutch Twins, Lucy touches upon proto-feminist ideas through a childish discussion between her twins about the ships sailing past them as the fish with their grandfather on the dyke near their home.

"I think I'll be a sea captain when I'm big," said Kit.
"So will I,", said Kat.
"Girls can't," said Kit.
But Grandfather shook his head and said: "You can't tell what a girl may be by the time she's four feet and a half high and is called Katrina. There's no telling what girls will do anyway."

This particular interest in Katrina's potential is reflected in Lucy's involvement in several social and artistic reform groups in Chicago, including the Chicago Women's Club and the League of Women Voters.

She saw the need for the themes of each story to be made vivid by their effect on the individuals involved. For Kit and Kat, young siblings growing up together and playing together, witnessing the ships sailing in front of them, the realisation of the female potential is made more vivid than if it were merely being explained to them in a classroom. By witnessing the ships sailing for America, England and elsewhere, Kat sees how the profession of sea-captain is a means for adventure and exploration, and so the injustice of the default, immediate "girls can't" is made painfully apparent. Similarly, to the American children reading the tale, since they can relate to the children's play and childishness, the messages is made more accessible. Lucy writes "I visited a school in Chicago where children of twenty-seven different nationalities were herded in one building, and marveled at what the teachers were able to accomplish. It seemed to me it might help in the fusing process if these children could be interested in the best qualities which they bring to our shores." Over two decades, Lucy wrote 26 stories in the Twins series. The popular children's author Beverly Cleary notes that the Twins series engaged her as an early reader, and ultimately served as inspiration for her writing. Alongside the Twins series, Lucy illustrated Edith Ogden Harrison's fairy tales, which were published in the 1900s.

As she well understood, it remains important to teach children early of the value of other cultures, and the history of one's own. Her writing can still be used as effective learning tools for their playful language, humour clarity still engages a young audience. Moreover, the sketches afford a visual representation of clothing and thereby a subtle hint at costume design for those children so enamoured with the stories that they wish to act them out. The Irish Twins, in particular, addresses "the abuses of absentee landlordism" which partly caused the mass immigration from Ireland to America at the country's birth.

Lucy died while holidaying in Pasadena, California, on 18th March 1937. She was seventy-two. Her books have been translated into several international languages, for their cultural importance is borderless. She writes that she "tried to contribute something to the making of Americans by an appreciation of what has been done in the past to make America what it is today, and of the constructive qualities in the material at hand with which we must build the nation of the future." This altruism and desire for social and cultural awareness and reform survives her, and though America went though almost a century of widespread social oppression, racism and xenophobia, as new writers and activists seek reform, we would do well to reflect on the pertinence and relevance of Perkins's work.

www.ingramcontent.com/pod-product-compliance
Lightning Source LLC
Chambersburg PA
CBHW061502170626
46811CB00004B/1592